Aim to Succeed

A novel

V S Mani

authorHOUSE®

AuthorHouse™ UK
1663 Liberty Drive
Bloomington, IN 47403 USA
www.authorhouse.co.uk
Phone: UK TFN: 0800 0148641 (Toll Free inside the UK)
        UK Local: 02036 956322 (+44 20 3695 6322 from outside the UK)

Published by AuthorHouse 07/25/2020

ISBN: 978-1-7283-5499-6 (sc)
ISBN: 978-1-7283-5500-9 (hc)
ISBN: 978-1-7283-5498-9 (e)

Print information available on the last page.

CONTENTS

PROLOGUE

It was a chilly morning with a temperature of around 10 degrees centigrade and a light breeze. It was lovely weather to walk around in and enjoy nature and the countryside. It was a typical spring day in Britain of 1955 – when it was usually cold with the probability of snow in the South East. Arun had certain routine chores to do for which he had to go to a shop nearby. He got into his car, a new model Austin Maxi estate and began driving, arriving at the shop, 15 minutes later.

He remembered that he had to get a card for Robin, who was leaving the neighborhood and migrating to the USA. He had known him for over eight years, on and off, always meeting him in restaurants or pubs; so far, each had not visited the other's apartment. Arun and Robin knew nothing of each other's parents or family.

Arun would be the first to admit that he was not a social person and was quite unusually shy. He was very observant but always kept his distance. He felt that familiarity might breed dislike with time. To preserve good relations, he preferred to err on the safe side and not get too close to people. Many had thought him cold and unfriendly. In reality, he was just the opposite. Pleasant manners and a courteous disposition were the hallmarks of his behavior. However, he took advantage of these negative views and kept himself as far from them as possible.

At the shop, he noticed a card on display with the words: 'How does one say goodbye to such a nice person?' Inside it was the words: "Reluctantly… very reluctantly." He chose it and began looking around for some other lovely items to gift as a token of their friendship. While doing so, he placed the card near the cashier. After a 15-minute search, he found a gold-plated beer mug with his friend's favorite football club, Manchester United's logo, inscribed on it. He took the item and placed it along with the card, catching the eye of the lady cashier. He indicated to her his intention to buy these two, after looking for some more items.

Arun, then, continued to browse to see if any more appropriate items to buy. He noticed two young girls enter the shop. One had stunning good looks and is dressed in a red skirt, a white blouse with a pretty blue scarf. The other girl was equally good-looking and appeared to be a few years younger. Probably a younger sister, Arun thought. Upon their entrance, the shop had the sweet fragrance of the perfume. Arun, though distracted, continued to look for another suitable item but, after a while, gave up and returned to the cash counter.

When he did, he was dismayed that the two items he had left there were missing. The gentleman at the cash desk said that the objects had was bought by one of the two ladies. When Arun protested, the man explained that many customers frequently discarded selected items at the billing counter. He asked Arun why he had not bothered to use the basket kept handy for shopping. He had assumed that the two things were discards and sold them to one of the young ladies a few minutes before. It turned out that the beautiful lady in her early twenties had paid for some items, including the card and beer mug, he had left on the counter.

On hearing this, Arun immediately approached her. "Excuse me, madam, you have bought the card and beer mug that I had left on the counter to purchase."

She looked at him angrily and said, "Excuse me, sir, I found the card and the beer mug abandoned on the counter and the cashier told me that he was going to place those back on the racks. Why don't you ask him if they have another card like this? Do sort out your gripe with the cashier and not with me!"

Arun said curtly, "I am sorry to have bothered you. All the time, I took to pick out an appropriate card and gift has been wasted. They do not have another card with such nice wording or a beer mug with the same logo."

"Tough luck," she shrugged unrepentantly, then quipped to her companion in a low voice that was still audible to others, "What cheek for a bloody nigger!"

Arun was more annoyed at her rudeness than the use of the racist 'nigger', and the remark about him being cheeky equally amazed him. She was an attractive young woman who appeared to be affluent, judging from the clothes she was wearing and had a polished accent. She was blonde, about 5'10 in height and had an erect bearing and a commanding stare. She had spoken to him, looking him straight in the eye, observing his reactions as she clearly and deliberately enunciated her words with intent to insult. She was not at all apologetic, but on reflection, Arun admitted that she did not have anything to apologize.

It was his mistake. He had assumed that the lady cashier had understood his intention to purchase the items. Perhaps he had been too hasty in blaming the woman. With all his education, as a medical doctor with further qualifications as an MD and Ph.D., he should have shown more restraint. After all, it was not the end of the world. There was still time to get another card and a gift before his friend's farewell party. As for the racist comment, he was used to hearing such remarks very frequently in London.

He apologized to the shopkeeper and his wife. The man joked, "The way you were looking at the elder girl… Despite your words, you were under her spell and would have willingly let her buy the items!" Arun smiled and felt a rush of blood to his cheeks.

The couple also said that they were sorry that the elder girl had made a racist remark Arun laughed, "It is better than kept bottled up." He was so used to hearing such comments in the big cities that he had become immune to it.

"Why didn't you respond?" the shopkeepers asked him. The girls who were still in the shop waited to hear what his reply would be. Arun said, "My education and experience have not trained me in the art of verbal garbage." The young couple listened but did not reply as they did not want to provoke further unpleasantness.

As more customers began were entering the shop, the shopkeepers left to attend to them. The girls left the shop with an angry look on their faces. Before leaving, the elder of the two girls angrily said: "I am shocked at the arrogant reply from a colored person – and that too in our own country!"

Arun, with a wry smile, left the shop, for his surgery, but could not forget the two girls. He wished he could meet them and apologize for his remarks and accusations. He felt he should buy them flowers or chocolates, as a peace offering, but another occasion to meet them might not arise. He had no anger towards the elder girl and felt sorry for her for holding such narrow, racist views.

CHAPTER 1

Village

Arun's thoughts switched to the day's tasks in the Surgery. He had a lot of patients to attend to, as John, the other GP, was on a leave of absence for a week, and Arun had to cover both the GP's appointment lists. Arun was the primary physician who owned the practice, and he had taken John on just a week ago, for two mornings a week. But John had hurt himself playing football, and he would be in plaster for at least a month.

Arun usually opened the Surgery at 8:30 AM and finished around 7:00 PM. He was single and lived in the apartment above the Surgery on the second floor. He had had this floor converted to accommodate two large self-contained flats, with a bedroom, an ensuite bathroom, and kitchen; on the first floor. There was another medium-sized apartment and a couple of rooms to serve as offices for all the staff with facilities for a copier, scanner, fax machine and other office equipment, and a small pantry. He intended to have the different GP live on the premises like him, but John did not want to do this as he wanted to be near the other GP practice where he worked three days a week.

Arun's Surgery was in a small village, which had a population of 4000 inhabitants. It was a remote village, and, until now, the residents had to journey 5-6 miles to find a GP. No GP had ventured to work for this small community. Arun had been working for five years in London, in a big private hospital, earning a very substantial income. He decided to come to the village as a GP, despite a considerable drop in his income. NHS HQ encouraged him to practice in the Village and offered him the right incentives for the relocation.

His NHS bosses had been very pleased with his sacrifice of income to serve the community. They gave a lot of incentives to modify the Surgery premises to suit his convenience. He was also allowed to practice, as an ophthalmic surgeon, at a nearby hospital, about 12 miles away. He planned to work there on his half-days on Wednesday afternoons and Saturdays and Sundays. The hospital would pay him for his services, as his private practice, outside the NHS income. His NHS bosses realized that in such a remote but affluent village, with mostly elderly patients, he would be expected to be a 24/7 GP and, hence, gave him generous incentives. These payments and perks could never make up for what he was earning as an ophthalmologist. However, he felt a commitment to this country and its people and agreed to relocate and serve the community. A few of the patients sometimes abused him verbally, mostly because of his color, but he always stood by his Hippocratic oath and served them all, despite their aggressive treatment of him.

He was a Hindu but always felt that since Britain followed Christianity, this had to be acknowledged and respected at all times. Being from India, his tolerance of Christians and Muslims came naturally. He had profound respect for all religions and their beliefs. However, he ensured that religion played no part in affecting his work ethic, and he would never allow it to do so.

When Arun had come to the village only the previous month, he had found a dilapidated Surgery, quite spacious but poorly maintained and not well equipped. It had a large garden, the front of which was overgrown with weeds and tall grass. He found no other place to stay in the village, and he waited for the Surgery to be modified for human occupation.

He visited the only shop there selling newspapers, groceries, drinks, and freshly baked goods. He thought the shop would be the right place to inquire about a plumber, electrician, gardener, etc. The owner, Mr. Dick Sanders, made it abundantly clear that he did not want people of color to frequent his shop, as his other customers might object, and his business would be affected.

In the face of his rudeness, Arun spoke up, "My name is Arun. I am the new GP for the village and have relocated from London. I would like help in getting skilled tradespeople to renovate the Surgery so that I can move in. Mr. Sanders, if I want certain items from your store each day and paid for them in advance, will you be able to supply or deliver them? Or, do I have to get one of my white employees to come and pick them up? I can pay a deposit now if you are agreeable, and when the credit runs out, I will top it up. Is that acceptable to you?"

Dick realized he had misjudged his customer and apologized, "Dr. Arun, I should not have spoken to you as I did. My family and I might need to visit you from time to time. I sincerely hope you will forgive me for the way I spoke to you earlier. I will accept your terms, and you can come into the shop anytime. I can also have an item delivered within an hour. Dave, who is a handyman, is seeking work, and Sandra and Debra, who were teachers, are also seeking work. You may use my office room – it is tiny – but you can conduct your interviews there. The room is at your disposal. Also, Doctor, please call me Dick and not Mr. Sanders."

Arun paid GBP 100 as a deposit and said, "I am most grateful for the introductions. I'm not able to order any provisions right now, except for the newspapers, as I have nowhere to stay till at least one room in the Surgery is made habitable."

Dick said, "Do not worry Doctor, we will not allow our GP to be homeless. Dave, his wife Sally, and I will make it livable by this evening. Do you have any luggage or furniture? When is your family expected? My wife Cathy will help as well if needed."

Arun said, "I have a sleeping bag and an air pillow modest but will suffice for now. I am single, and that simplifies matters. Each of the three consulting rooms should have a bed, and he wanted one of those for tonight."

Dick offered tea and croissants for Arun to take and sent his young son, Martin, to fetch Dave, Sally, Sandra and Debra immediately. Astonishingly, they all arrived quickly.

Arun was lucky to find Dave, a DIY specialist, who did not have

3

enough work in such a small village and did not have the transport to seek employment in nearby communities. Arun employed him full-time, as a caretaker and an odd-jobs man. He also employed Sally as a housekeeper and to work in the garden. Sally was a keen gardener and an able cook and did various other chores, including house cleaning. Arun offered her and her husband Dave good salaries.

He also gave Dave money to buy a second-hand van to carry his tools and use for transport. For Dave and Sally, Arun did a full health check to ensure they had no ailments and found that both were in good health. Both being very active by doing hard physical work every day, they had kept their bodies in good shape.

Sandra and Debra, he hired as receptionists. In their mid-forties, they were both spinsters who lived together in a small bungalow. They had been teachers earlier, but when the local school closed four years ago, no other jobs were available. They immediately accepted the offer of work from Arun. He assured them that their jobs were permanent positions and he expected them to treat the patients well and refrain from uttering words or remarks about color or race. They agreed readily to those stipulations.

Through Sandra and Debra, Arun met Mary and Dennis. They were also appointed. Mary, nearly 58, was employed as a part-time Medical Secretary – she was good at typing and shorthand and had previously worked for a large corporation, in one of the big cities. She had come to live in the village following her husband Dennis's early retirement at 60. Dennis was a retired accountant and Arun managed to get him to work in the Surgery as an accountant, for a modest salary. Dennis could choose his hours of work and he was glad to take care of stores by checking orders and receipts.

Arun did not anticipate that the work in the Surgery and essential recruitment of staff could be done so quickly and that the Surgery would look so clean shortly after his lengthy instructions to Dave. Now, all it needed was a fresh coat of paint and Dave would sort that out first before embarking on the garden with Sally. In two weeks, the Surgery looked immaculate and people in the village began wondering what was happening. Arun did not meet anyone other than the staff he had appointed and Dick's family, and he kept a low profile. Consequently, no one knew of Arun, as the local GP. They viewed him as a colored visitor who might go away in a few days. Arun had requested Dick not to say anything till the Surgery was fully ready and Dick had obliged.

All were asked to keep the news under the hat until the Surgery was fully tidied up and ready for patients. Mary prepared notices about the Surgery's opening with the proposed date and timings. She also announced this in a local village meeting, to which Arun had not been invited. Arun also met the managers of the only bank in the village, a real estate agency, and a small Post Office.

Dick was very proud that he had helped to get the Doctor settled in the village and the Surgery opened for local inhabitants. Many were not happy. They would have preferred a white GP and they also knew that none had wanted to come.

Arun started the practice, appointing John for two mornings a week. The patient booking was modest for the first few days but increased by the end of the week. He fully understood and appreciated the efforts taken by Dick, his wife Cathy, and all his staff. Dave and Sally gave a nice impression that it was the village surgery and Arun was just the GP working there at present. They did not know that the Surgery owed a lot to Arun more than anyone else. Till now no doctor had wanted to work in a village this small.

Within a week, John had been incapacitated. Arun's morning patients were routine coughs and colds and he was able to clear the appointments of two GPs by 1:00 PM. He then saw the letters left on his desk by the receptionists, one of which he realized was from John. He opened the letter to find that John had decided to call it a day as far as working for this Surgery was concerned, as he had an offer to do all five days in the other Surgery. So that was the end of that chapter.

Arun had two immediate requirements – one, was for a dependable GP whom he could take on as a full partner in four years, as long as he/she committed to the practice and to make a long-term career in this small village, and second, was for a young and good Practice Manager. He was prepared to accept, even a male to fill the post, normally a job done by a female. For the present, Mary was also doing the senior receptionists' job – making appointments and overseeing the two receptionists. She was well aware that once a Practice Manager was appointed she would no longer be needed to fill the present role.

Arun had his lunch, had a kip for 20 minutes and then, before the clinic started, he wanted to draft and check the adverts for a GP and a Practice Manager. He wrote in detail about the small village atmosphere so that no applicant was misled. When he was finally satisfied with their wording, he placed the adverts in all the medical magazines, knowing fully well that no one would apply. The small village was out of their radar.

CHAPTER 2

Preparation

Three weeks rolled by, and as expected, there were no responses. Arun had not expected any. He used the Wednesday afternoon off-day to do three operations in the hospital for ophthalmology and six procedures each on Saturdays and Sundays. On one of these days, he bought a suitable card and a present for Robin, in anticipation of his farewell party.

Eventually, he received a telegram from his friend, stating, "I had to leave urgently for the USA due to job requirements, so there will be no party – sorry." Arun was deeply disappointed, as he wanted to see his friend before he left. The news brought back to memory the incident in the shop with the two girls. With a wry smile, he returned to his patients. To decorate, the Surgery receptionists chose pleasing colors. The kitchen was immaculate and fitted with minimal equipment, as per Arun's choice. He told Sally that he was a Hindu, very occasionally an egg-vegetarian, and did not eat garlic. His selection of food was quite simple; stir-fried vegetables, minimal spices cooked in olive oil, South Indian filter coffee twice a day. Use of Oxo cubes or lard discouraged. He was conscious of his health and wanted to eat sensibly to avoid diabetes later in life. For exercise, he walked and ran frequently.

He had given Dave and Sally instructions about planting a border of flowers with full paving slabs all around the interior of the edge so that anyone could walk or run within the garden. He did not want to run outside and attract public attention and listen to rude remarks at him. Since Dave had installed the paving slabs, Arun had been doing 40 laps, every morning and evening.

Sally had not only planted flowers selected to bloom at various times of the year, but also used potted plants in the front, to make the Surgery look attractive when people passed by.

The clinics were also well equipped due to the quick delivery of items that Arun had pre-ordered before coming to the village. These also included instruments and equipment for ophthalmology clinics and operations about the eye. A third consultation room accommodated Arun's specialty. His long-term goal, in 5-6 years, was to have a separate clinic near the village for ophthalmology and a nursing home for convalescing patients. He managed to get the old ambulance serviced and repaired. Dave test-drove the ambulance for an hour and found it to be reliable for emergency trips. It saved Arun the expense of buying a new one, though a new one would have had better features.

Arun was able to get the patient list of the previous GP who had practiced there about six years ago. He found, after comparing it with the list of present inhabitants, that most of them were still resident in the village. Aware of strong feelings running against him from very influential members of the community, Arun decided to use as a front, Mary, and Dennis. They were held in very high esteem by the residents of the village. A few of the residents had died, but there was also an influx of new, young inhabitants. He then asked his staff to group the inhabitants into categories such as age, gender, occupation, and social class. He was able to discern from the patient attendance, that families belonging to the higher level did not come to the Surgery and were probably opting to go to the nearest cities for private healthcare. Or, perhaps they were quite healthy and did not need to visit the GP as frequently as the others did.

Two extremely affluent families were identified, who did not mix with the rest – but they provided an income to some skilled people in the village. This type of help by them was considered far more critical, and their lack of socializing did not matter to them. Perhaps the others felt that if they too had such abundant wealth, they might also behave similarly. These two families lived in stately homes with an estate of

100-150 acres of land fenced for security and privacy. No outsider was ever allowed in without prior permission from the owners.

Arun discovered that the two families had made a lot of money – the Howard family from diamond mines in Botswana, and the Richard family from gold mines in South Africa. They were old buddies, perhaps related, and decided to settle down in the village, leaving one or two of their offspring to manage their mines in Africa. Their employees had strict instructions not to discuss with anyone, their occupations, wealth, and any other details. As the two families provided the village with enough money for general upkeep and all utilities, they were well respected. There were six other families, quite well off, but not like the Howard's and the Richard's. They did socialize, but they had not visited the Surgery even once. Unlike the other two families, details for these families were readily available. The rest of the population was mostly middle class and about 20% as having low income and not having a living wage. Arun felt sorry for them but had no way to improve their lot immediately.

Arun arranged an Open Day for the Surgery and gave out leaflets about the services provided, the staff at present, and ancillary staff like Dave and Sally.

Before that, Arun trained all the staff with dummy questions and scripted responses to be provided by the team. All visitors were shown around the Surgery by his staff, and snacks and drinks provided for the visitors. There was a question-answer session as well. The visitors were quite happy with the information. Many said that even in inner cities, such details not given out, as the GPs kept their distance. They felt Arun's approach was very open and extremely helpful.

Arun was disappointed that despite the large number of people who visited the Surgery, the two ladies he met in the shop, were not there. Perhaps they were passing through the village. Or, they might belong to either the Howard or Richard family, in which case he might never see them. He did know a lot of new faces who had not come to the Surgery so far.

Arun felt the response to the Open Day had been better than expected. He had befriended many local, influential people, and they thought that he was one of them – not to refer as colored or a nigger. They knew that they owed him a lot to choose to come to the village and take over the Surgery. He felt he had a status in the community within a short time and won their confidence and trust. Him being the GP and an ophthalmologist and providing a dedicated healthcare service with a happy disposition earned him laurels quickly. However, he had to turn down the opportunity to serve on the council due to his surgery work.

Arun felt the Surgery might get busy with such a large turnout for the Open Day, and he needed to find a Practice Manager and a nurse soon. He was at a loss to know how to go about it. His contacts in London were of no help, as people did not want to relocate to such a small village in a remote part of the UK.

Arun had read widely about Hinduism, the Bible new and old testaments, and extracts from the Koran, Taoism, Buddhism, Jainism, and the Sikh religion. He felt that they all preached the same message about being a good human being. Despite this, religious wars persisted. The main word Arun had derived from his readings was that one has to surrender to the Supreme. Arun felt that he needed such faith to find suitable staff for the Surgery, as the work intended was for humanity's common good. He strongly felt that God would not let him down in his mission to serve his fellow human beings.

Arun thought of the Arabic poem he had read in India when he was a young boy – Abu Ben Adam. The poem was about a king who noticed an angel in his bedroom, writing something. When he asked, the angel replied that he was writing down 'the names of those who love God.' The king asked, "Is my name there?" The angel answered that his name was not on the list. Disappointed, the king requested humbly, "Will you please put my name on the list of those who love their countrymen?" The next night, the king asked whether the angel had completed the list. The angel replied, "I have completed the list, and your name is at the top of the list of people who love God." The implication was that if you love your fellow human beings, it is equivalent to loving God.

Arun felt that his mission had to be successful and that God would show him the way. Another week passed by, and there were no responses. This time, he repeated the adverts for the Practice Manager, a GP and a nurse in the local papers, only covering an area of 25 miles radius, and suggested that elderly applicants, who had retired early, might also apply. The adverts appeared a few days later, and the following Monday, he had three applicants, one for each post.

CHAPTER 3

The Unexpected

Arun was quite pleased that the last round of adverts had borne some fruit and he was reminded of the Indian politician, Mr. Rajaji's reply to an American Journalist after Mr. Rajaji came out of a meeting with the then President, John F. Kennedy, after a nuclear disarmament discussion. On being asked whether the discussions were fruitful, he replied that he would say they were flowerful as he did not know whether these flowers would bear any fruit. Arun felt grateful that at least he had some applicants and opened the letters. To his surprise, there was a middle-aged lady applying for the post of an administrator, a young lady of 27 applying for the advertised post of Practice Manager and another young lady of 25 applying for the post of a nurse. Their details reasonably matched the specifications needed, so he asked Mary to fix their interviews for the following week.

Arun did not notice the applicants' names as he felt that he would be seeing them anyway the following week, but in his mind, he fixed the name Barbara for an administrative post, Elizabeth for Practice Manager and Christine for the post of a nurse. He also did not notice the various addresses, in his head.

He had, in the advert, mentioned the name of the surgery and the GP's name appeared as Dr. A. Ayer. This surname, he found quite useful in the UK, as some of the British people had the same surname. He had changed his name by Deed Poll on arrival to the UK about six years ago. He felt that with strong feelings running high in those days, particularly against people of color, the surname, Iyer, used in India might not go down well, and so spelt it as Ayer. Many a time he had been mistaken as British on applications for a consultant post and witnessed a very surprised look from the interviewers. However, his quality of work had carried the day, as he had done well in London and got meritorious certificates and honors in the field.

On Saturday, Arun had to go to a small town nearby to pick up some books which he had ordered earlier. He liked to read up a lot on medicine, history, philosophy, fiction and Westerns. He liked Western movies too, as they are very predictable – good triumphs over evil, dialogues are simple and go to the core of basic human nature. Being away from a big city, he felt ordering books in advance and collecting them was the prudent option. The journey to the nearest small town involved using a country road with sporadic passing places. The road was generally not wide enough for two cars to use. One had to drive very slowly to avoid collisions – even 40 mph is excessive on such a road. Sounding the horn is not usually done, unlike countries in the Far East – India in particular. The winding narrow road had overgrown hedges on both sides and if a driver went too close to the hedge, then the car would get scratched and incur exorbitant repair costs.

While driving to the town, he chose a country lane as it saved about six miles. He had not driven through the lane before, so he was exceedingly careful. He noticed two large brick-walled compounds enclosing a large acreage of land and castle-like properties with several outbuildings on them. He also noticed a number of workmen on each property. There were metal gates with a security guard monitoring them periodically. There were no names on the walls near the entrance gates. The rest of the areas, beyond the compounds, were fields used for farming and the farmhouses set quite far away from the lane. A low fence covered the grounds used by the farmer. Arun did not meet with any traffic while going and he thought he was either lucky or no one else had wanted to use the lane.

Arun parked the car in the quaint little town, walked on the High

Street to look at the shops and the things they sold. He came to the bookshop and waited until the cashier was free. The shopkeeper recognized him and brought him a package containing the books and other items that he had ordered and took the money due. Arun thanked him for the service provided and left. As he emerged he saw a red sports car, open-top, with two young ladies driving at a speed exceeding the limits imposed, whizzing past. He did not get a chance for more than a fleeting look but heard some villagers muttering about the arrogance of youth and money. Very briefly Arun wondered whether these two ladies could be the ones he met in the shop but dismissed the thought as he felt he was obsessed with wanting to meet them, to apologize for his rude behavior.

It was nearly mid-day. Arun found the only café in town, chose a table with only two seats and sat down facing the door. He looked at the menu and nothing appealed to him. He, therefore, ordered a bowl of tomato soup, followed by a couple of sandwiches with cucumber, tomato and a little cheese. Being a teetotaler, he ordered plain water. There was a rush of customers entering the shop and to his surprise he saw the sports car pull up outside and the two ladies walked into the café. They did not see him at first but when they sat down a few tables away he was in their sightline. The elder one whispered something to the younger one and immediately the younger woman turned around to see him. Arun noticed the exchanges between the two ladies but was hesitant to address them. He found both girls to be very good-looking, but the elder one was especially dashing!

Arun always carried his briefcase with him, even on casual occasions like this. His underlying belief was that emergency situations could arise at any time and, a doctor should always be prepared. As he was waiting for the soup to be served, he opened the case discreetly, took out a plain sheet of paper and wrote the following:

Dear ladies,

I am writing to apologize very sincerely to both of you. You may remember I met you both in a shop a few days ago, where I went to buy a card and a present – a beer mug, which I could not buy. In frustration,

I uttered words which I have since regretted. It was stupid of me to say the things I did. In the heat of the moment, I lost my composure.

Please accept my heartfelt apologies. I would like to buy a box of chocolates and a bouquet of flowers as a token of my gratitude to you both and sincerely hope that you overlook that incident. I assure you that it will never happen again.

With kind regards,

Arun

He folded the letter, put it in an envelope and addressed it to:

Two lovely ladies

From: *A very stupid person – Sorry!*

He requested the waitress who served the soup to give the envelope to the two ladies and showed her the table where they were sitting. She delivered the envelope and came back to say that the errand had been done, as requested.

The elder of the two ladies on receipt of the envelope glanced at him and Arun hesitated but did not acknowledge that he had sent it. She then opened the letter, read it, and passed it on to her friend, who also read it and glanced back at him. They did not say anything, nor did they reply to him. After an hour had passed since the note had been delivered, Arun felt that it was better to leave the café as he had other chores to take care of in town. As he passed the table where the ladies were still drinking coffee, they averted their gaze, which he understood as 'not interested' and he walked hurriedly to his car.

Arun, as a person, did not allow any misunderstandings to persist for a prolonged duration and he always made peace with the person, even if it was not his fault. He would have preferred to buy them the flowers and chocolates and then forget them for good, but such a solution had been denied to him in this case. Whenever his colour became an issue, he always kept a low profile and he had to presume, from the comment made by the elder of the two on that day, that his apology had done nothing to change her opinion.

With an air of resignation, he proceeded with the other chores he had planned, which occupied him for another hour, after which he began driving back cautiously through the country lanes, back to his surgery.

CHAPTER 4

Another View

Elizabeth and Christine Howard were sisters, daughters of Mr. Jeff Howard, and Barbara. Jeff had inherited his father's diamond mines in Botswana, which is one of the wealthiest countries. People mistakenly assume South Africa, with its gold mines, is the most prosperous country in Africa. Jeff lived in Botswana, in the lap of luxury. He was used to thinking of the workers as 'niggers.' Due to poverty, lack of sanitation, education, and food, masses of people lived with the shame of being addressed in such derogatory terms. If they got a job, then their lot improved, and this prevented them from rioting. They lived with apartheid, practiced commonly in all the African countries. The practice of addressing black people as niggers over the years applied to all people, black or brown, including those from the Indian subcontinent

Jeff inherited the property at the age of 25 when his father passed away due to a local uprising, as he was ruthless in the treatment of the locals. He had to change his ways lest he would meet his Waterloo and exactly he met with a violent death. After a year of uncertainty, the police restored normalcy, and Jeff introduced changes to the working practices and treatment of the locals. His first wife, Sheila, born in the UK but brought up in Botswana, had a disability, and after Jake was born, she died within a year. Jeff then married Barbara, on visiting the UK and choosing his bride from Cornwall. After ten long years, Elizabeth was born and Christine two years later. Liz and Chris were mostly brought up in Cornwall, as Barbara preferred to stay on in the UK, due to the political unrest in South Africa. She found the rampant racism in South Africa and Botswana repugnant. Consequently, she did not have much involvement with the upbringing of Jake apart from the earlier years. Once the girls were born, Jake decided to live with this dad in Botswana, and Barbara opted to live in Cornwall.

Jeff was a pleasant character, very modest and sympathetic, and treated his workers fairly. The girls used to visit Botswana during their school holidays. Liz, always exuding arrogance because of her beauty and wealth, inherited her late grandfather's bad manners, and treated the locals with derision. Calling people niggers came naturally to her. Chris was more understanding, lovable, and kind, and her nature attracted more people. When she was ten, she objected to Liz addressing people of color as niggers, as their mother Barbara had forbidden them from using the term. However, Liz would not listen, and while her parents hoped her nature would change with age, it never happened. Chris was always loyal to her sister on all issues except this one. She did not want to openly quarrel with her sister because she thought Liz would become alienated, and then there would be no one to institute a change in Liz. Other people misconstrued her silence on many occasions, and Chris got into their bad books. Many local people in the UK also did not like Liz using the term, as the UK was supporting Nelson Mandela, who was unfairly imprisoned by the South African government. Chris was sure that Liz would learn a lesson one of these days.

Jake had managed his dad's investments from the age of 25 and was doing very well. Ultimately Jeff, too, decided to stay in the UK and lead a retired life. They lived in a significant estate in the small village. Richards family owned in a similar large estate but rarely stayed long in the UK.

Jeff and Barbara had their mansion within the compound wall. Barbara's parents also lived in the village. Both the houses were fully staffed with 20 workers, from Head Cook to gardeners. They all lived within the compound and rarely visited the Village or the Town, except on special occasions.

After leaving the gift shop, totally flustered, Liz told Chris that she could not stand 'that colored man's arrogance and comments.' Chris said that she did not think he was arrogant and thought any rudeness might stem from his frustration arising from the misunderstanding with the shopkeeper. Liz said, "I know you will always take the opposite view to mine! I know I am right in this case."

They drove to the house without speaking a word. Liz narrated the incident with high intensity and anger when her mother asked the girls why they were so angry and what had happened. Barbara used to Liz's dramatics, raised an eyebrow at Chris, who said that the narrative was far from the truth, and it was a mistake precipitated by the shop owner. She also said that Liz's racist comments were unnecessary.

Barbara sighed. Liz was 27 and was beyond being prompted on courtesy. She frequently warned Liz that she would, one day, get her comeuppance. Still, Liz had always laughed it off and said, 'not in my lifetime.' Liz was very good in her studies and art, was quite fashionable, and had a brilliant way of decorating a house, an office, or even public places for meetings and fetes. Her ideas were innovative, and she was very resourceful in an emergency. Liz could not bear to take orders from anyone and liked to be the boss. She worked for a short while in a local bank in the village, and she got into an argument with the Bank Manager. As a front desk cashier, her role was minimal. She would act as if she was the Manager and advise the customer accordingly. Within a short time, she left the bank, despite her father being one of their biggest account holders. She had not worked since, though she was good at admin-related work. She needed careful guidance of her energies, and she needed to learn restraint. Liz's treatment of local workers, even whites, was far from satisfactory. She annoyed people and, in general, they feared and sometimes even loathed her. They wished she would go back to Africa.

Chris, on the other hand, was gentle, very easy going, courteous, soft-spoken, respected everyone, and addressed all in a very civil manner. She was good-looking, stylish as Liz, rarely used make-up, and was extremely intelligent. She was 25 and had trained to be a nurse and wanted to work in a Medical Practice.

Barbara did not want the girls to move to big cities like London,

Birmingham, Liverpool, and Manchester. With enough money in a Trust Fund to satisfy five generations, the need to work was not paramount, but she felt some work was necessary to keep their minds busy. All youngsters in the current age were working, earning, and enjoying life, and did not want the girls to miss out on the experience. She hoped they would find work locally.

Liz and Chris were pleasantly surprised to see the local newspaper advertisement for the posts of a GP, a nurse, and a Practice Manager. Liz fancied the job as a Practice Manager, and Chris was happy to apply for a nurse's position. They applied for the posts on the same day and addressed it to Dr. A. Ayer, as the advert stated. They were surprised to receive an immediate response from the Surgery about an interview the following Wednesday. Barbara was more excited, and she offered to come to the surgery with them on the day of the meeting, but the girls refused. The stress of having their mother and her expectations would be too much for them. They felt an opportunity such as this might not arise in such a small village. Barbara did not tell the girls that she also had applied for the admin job.

Liz and Chris wanted to go to town to buy some clothes, and Liz took the convertible sports car. Chris wanted to drive, as she was a very safe and not a Speedy Gonzales like Liz. But Liz would have none of it. It was her car, and she wanted to drive. Chris had not wanted a sports car, as the Village did not have roads to drive such a vehicle. She had a new model Mini for secure parking and suitable for narrow lanes. They eventually agreed to take Liz's sports car into town, where Liz picked up some designer clothing. Chris usually did not buy clothes from such expensive stores. She was not a trendsetter – or even a follower of fashion. Her professional education and experience had taught her to view life from a different perspective.

After shopping, they had gone to a café where Liz immediately noticed the man that she and Chris had exchanged unpleasant words. They took their seats in the restaurant and felt uneasy seeing him there. Chris did not feel wrong about the man being in the café and realized that they had to meet him off and on if he lived in the area. She told Liz not to harp on his presence.

To their surprise, the waitress taking orders brought a letter from the man. The address at the top and the details inside astonished them. The very politely written, and Arun, whose name they only knew from the letter, had made it look as if it was his mistake entirely and apologized. He did not blame the shop owner or Liz for any words she had used. He even went to the extent of offering to buy flowers and a box of chocolates. Liz unconvinced by the apology and said that it might be his excuse to befriend them and that they should avoid him at all costs.

Liz and Chris had to accept that Arun, who was about 6 ft tall, was quite handsome, with a complexion more whitish than brown. "Maybe he is from North India, they thought, rather than the hotter regions of the South." He was very smartly dressed and exuded an air of confidence but not arrogance. He seemed like a person anyone would like to be friendly.

Chris wanted to reply to Arun, but Liz would have none of it. She did not want Chris to cave in because Arun was handsome. Liz told Chris not to talk any more about Arun or his letter or their response and insisted that they ignore him. So, they did just that. After Arun left, they also left. Liz had a feeling he might stop and talk to them. If he did, she told Chris, she would not have minded.

"You hypocrite," laughed Chris, "you are so against him but still want his attention. You are mesmerized by his looks but do not want to admit it. Also, you do not care about his color even though you refer to it, more as a diversion to mask your attraction."

They came out to find that Arun was no longer there, and they both felt for the missed opportunity. They bought a few more things and then started for home. Liz wanted to reach home early to watch a serial. She started the car at high speed to return home. Chris told her to go slow, but Liz would have none of it. It only made her accelerate more.

CHAPTER 5

Less Haste, More Speed

Arun finished his work in town and started to drive back to the Surgery. As he approached the small lane, he slowed down further, in case a vehicle was coming in the opposite direction. There were several bends, which meant he had to drive extremely slowly. He was driving much slower than the required speed limit, but as there was no traffic behind him, he was happy to proceed safely. And suddenly, a sports car appeared behind him, and the driver repeatedly honked, urging him to move out. In his mirror, he saw that a lady was behind the wheel with a companion in the passenger seat. He hand-signaled (so that they should slow down) by lowering his car window, but the honking did not stop. He tried to speed up to the next available passing zone, and when he finally found one, he made room for the vehicle to pass.

The car stopped, parallel to his, and the driver shouted, "Why do you drive so slowly, like an old man? People like you should go back to your own country and drive bullock carts, not cars like civilized people!"

Arun just smiled and said, "I will bear that in mind, but until I get a ticket to go back, I would like to use a car."

Arun continued, "Please don't travel at high speeds in this small lane. The visibility is poor, and you may have an accident causing injury to you and damage to the car. Please drive more carefully. Now that you can go ahead of me, you will not find anyone uncivilized ahead to slow you down."

Liz said, "Despite your apology, you are still arrogant and sarcastic. I know very well how to drive. You nigger! You just want some excuse to talk to two white girls. I know your kind very well. Keep your apologies and warnings to yourself!"

Arun was upset that the elder girl was using such racist language, but he kept his cool and said, "My apology is genuine. I wanted to deliver it personally, but the opportunity never arose. When I left, I had no idea that I would meet up with you both, and so soon. I'm sorry if you misunderstood my intentions and got upset."

Liz snorted derisively, "I do not trust people like you and do not believe a word of what you say. I hope we never meet again!" So, saying she rushed off at high speed, showing her middle finger to him, as she drove past.

Arun had never been so humiliated in his life before and felt immensely disheartened. He was at a loss as to why his behavior and comments were causing such outrage. He thought that what the lady said might be right about his sounding sarcastic without realizing it. He seemed to be creating a lot of unnecessary annoyance. Despite these bad feelings, he tried to calm down and started the car to proceed to his Surgery.

As he was driving along, he heard a big bang. Suddenly he remembered the two ladies in the sports car and prayed it was not an accident, as he had predicted. He traveled a mile or so and found the very thing he dreaded. He quickly parked his car, placed two large stones on the road, well behind his vehicle, so that no one could come at a speed and ram into it. He then rushed to inspect the accident scene.

The car had crashed into a large tree on the driver's side, and the driver had blood oozing from injuries to the head, face, and neck, and was unconscious. He checked the pulse, and it was feeble. The other lady in the passenger seat was hurt and shaken and had a concussion. She had no external injuries.

He switched off the sports car and took the key. He walked a few feet in front of the accident zone and placed two large stones to stop oncoming vehicles.

He brought his briefcase and gave the driver an injection to sedate her and to reduce the pain. He then found that the driver's legs were free with the wreckage. He left her, as she was, and went to attend to the younger girl. Her pulse rate was slightly low, but her breathing was normal but labored. He tried to wake her up. When she opened her eyes, he asked her where she lived. She said she lived in the house with a large compound. He wondered whether it was the first or the second house. She said second. He then opened the boot and all the doors of his car and lifted the driver and rested her on one side. Her shoes fell off, which he picked up and put it near her. He then lifted the younger girl and put her next to the older girl. He then shut the doors and locked the car. He removed the stones he had placed on the road and started looking for the second house with a compound wall. He pressed the bell, and the gates opened. He drove through the long driveway until he came to the sizeable castle-type house.

Barbara heard the sound of voices and came outside, just as Arun was telling the security men of the accident. She was immediately worried and asked what happened. Arun introduced himself as a Medical Doctor and said that he had given the elder girl a sedative as she was bleeding and in pain. The younger one had a concussion. He wanted them to be taken in and put on two adjacent beds, on the ground floor so that he could take care of them during the night. Barbara's husband, Jeff, came out, and she explained it to him briefly.

Arun assured them that he would explain everything later on, but for now, he had to focus on the patients. He wanted to use their phone to get help from his Surgery. When they showed him the phone, he called Dave and asked him and Sally to come to an address which the owners would direct them. He wanted Dave to bring the ambulance and ensure that the supplies were in their compartments. He wanted Sally to bring her car in case she or Dave had to make a few trips to the Surgery. Arun wanted the ambulance left outside the house. He then passed the phone to Barbara, who gave directions to Dave and said that some of the staff would be waiting for them near the locked gate to let them in.

The maid arrived with two ladies to help and said that the beds had been prepared and ready. They also brought two cots outside. Arun carefully placed the elder girl on one of the cots and asked the ladies to take her gently to the bedroom. They carefully put her and her companion on the two beds set up on the ground floor. He wanted the two lady attendants to stay with him for about an hour to help with various chores.

He asked everyone to leave except for the two lady attendants and asked them to change the girls' clothing to nightdresses without lifting their arms or legs unduly. If that was not possible, then the nightgowns had to be slit right from top to bottom at the back and put on from the front.

He left the room to find out whether Dave and Sally had arrived. Barbara told Arun that the elder sister was called Elizabeth, known as Liz, and the younger one was Christine, known as Chris. Arun thanked her for the introduction and noticed the arrival of the ambulance. He, Barbara, and her husband went out to meet Dave and Sally. Arun then checked the supplies and took out some essentials needed immediately and told Sally to note each item taken and to bring the stock to the usual level.

Arun went to the bedroom and cleaned the wounds of Liz and Chris. He then set up one drip unit for Liz and one for Chris; these were glucose feed, and the strength used for Liz was double that of Chris, as Liz had significant injuries and was bleeding. He also set up pulse and BP monitors to keep a watch through the night. He observed that when the car hit the tree, it looked like she had risked herself to protect her younger companion. The steering wheel had protected her but had caused injuries to her forehead and face with severe lacerations and bleeding. She had also just evaded a thick branch piercing through the glass that would have gone through her heart. It was her good luck that she had escaped such a death.

He asked the staff to bring a bed or a reclining chair and place it in between Liz and Chris so that he could keep an eye on them during the night.

Barbara said one of the girls in her employ could be on the vigil, but Arun said he had experience of doing the night shifts in hospitals and was quite alert to small noises. He said the girl could also stay if Barbara wanted, but he must be in the same room as Liz and Chris that night until they got through the critical period. Arun said that Chris should be awake and should be all right in about 5-6 hours, but Liz might take longer to recover. By morning he said that she should be able to talk and make some sense.

Arun called the nearest hospital to report the accident saying he was present immediately after. He told them the two patients are being looked after by him in their home. He had set up precautionary glucose drips, and he was monitoring their pulse and BP continually. The hospital staff knew him well and were relieved that the girls were receiving prompt attention. They felt the patients were in safe hands, and they conveyed this to Jeff and Barbara. Arun promised to update the hospital staff, as required.

Arun said, "Mrs. and Mr. Howard, I need to tell you a long story about how we three met under three different circumstances, all unplanned, without even exchanging names. I came to know Liz and Chris only through Mrs. Howard a few minutes ago. I never knew who they were, where they lived, and whether they were friends or sisters. I will tell you my side of the story; I am sure in due course Liz will share her version." Arun then narrated the incidents, as they had happened until he brought them to their home. He said the sisters probably did not know that he was the new GP. He also said that he was an ophthalmologist who practiced in the hospital in town a few days a week.

The Howards were dumbfounded to know that there was so much history behind each other's three meetings, and they were sorry that Liz had insulted him. They were extremely grateful to him for bringing them home and taking good care of them, overlooking the racist remarks. Whether their daughters were grateful or not, they would be eternally indebted to him.

"Please call us, Barbara and Jeff," Barbara said. She insisted that

Arun have dinner with them. When Sally pointed out that Arun was a vegetarian and only occasionally ate eggs, Barbara summoned her chef and asked him to prepare food for the doctor as per Sally's instructions. She had the feeling that the doctor might be sharing many a future meal with them.

CHAPTER 6

They also serve, who stand and wait.

(From 'On His Blindness' by John Milton)

After his simple dinner with the Howards, Arun came to the bedroom and found the pulse rate and BP readings were returning to normal for both ladies. He told Barbara and Jeff that the girls would be okay in a few hours medically but might not remember all the details of the accident immediately. By noon tomorrow, they might be able to relate what happened. Barbara and Jeff told Arun that they would wait in the bedroom for a couple of hours or so until 11:00 PM and then go to bed, leaving Arun to look after his patients during the night. He should be able to call on one of the two attendants assigned to help him during the night.

It was 9:00 PM, and the house was getting to be quiet, as all the staff had left for their homes within the compound, and a skeleton staff of five, in rotation every week, usually slept inside the house.

Barbara asked Arun whether he needed any pajamas, but Arun said that he had to be in work clothes whenever he was on night duty. Changing into pajamas might relax him and affect his critical thinking faculties. Barbara made arrangements for a coffee percolator in the room. They sat together but did not talk much, as Arun was continually monitoring progress, checking his patient's breathing, and updating comments on their charts.

Around 10:00 PM, Chris opened her eyes, and the first person she saw was Arun. She said, "You again? Why are you here? Where is Liz?" Barbara and Jeff rushed to her, and on seeing their faces, Chris was relieved. Barbara said, "Arun is a doctor. He was the first to arrive on the scene of the accident and brought both of you here. Liz had severe cuts, and she bled a lot, but she is getting better."

Chris said, "Thank you, doctor. We have been extremely rude to you whenever we met, and it was nice of you to overlook that and treat us, for which I am very grateful." Arun said that those incidents were in the past, and what was needed was for her to get better quickly. Her mum reached out to hug her, but Arun said, "Let me make it easier for you," and removed all the tubes and sensors. Barbara then embraced Chris and started to cry. Jeff also did the same; they hated to see Chris laid up in bed. Arun assured them that her faculties would not be affected, despite the concussion. They were delighted to hear that, and so was Chris.

She declared, "I never knew you were such a lovely person. What a stupid mistake we made. How racist we were. I am very sorry about that. I did tell Liz she should not use such racist words, but she is a law unto herself – I love everything about her, except that."

Arun said, "Thank you, but for now, please focus on your recovery. Have some soup and bread, and then get some sleep. If you have any headache or body pain, let me know. I will be staying with you both during the night."

Chris suddenly looked at her dress and blushed. "Did you change my dress?"

Barbara said, "No, he asked one of the maids to change, but he advised her to slit the nightdress and put it on." Chris was happy to hear that, but her cheeks got a bit redder. She sat on the bed after Arun adjusted the pillows, and when she was nearly upright, the maid gave the tray to her.

After that light meal, Chris wanted to go to sleep, and Arun put back all the tubes and sensors, except the glucose drip, as she had already started eating healthy food. At 11:00 PM, the Howards thanked him again, stating how happy they were to find Chris recovered and able to eat and drink. They left after asking him to call them when Liz woke up or if he needed anything.

When Barbara and Jeff entered their bedroom, Barbara said, "What a day! It was so shocking. Instead of seeing the girls coming home laughing and showing off their shopping, they end up coming bloody and unconscious!"

Jeff said, "True, dear! It was a painful few hours. I was glad the doctor was the one to spot them and bring them home,"

Barbara said, "You are right, dear. At first sight, I did not think much of the young man and assumed he was chasing white girls. When Arun introduced himself as a medical doctor, I started to think of him differently. The way he took care of them – from his car to their beds, set up test equipment and sensors, and talked to the police and the hospital – made me rue my snap judgment of him. I felt very ashamed of my judgmental views based on the color of the person, even though I rarely voice it as Liz does."

Jeff said, "I feel the same way. When Chris spoke about how Liz made racial slurs but that the doctor had taken it in his stride, that told me a lot about him. It makes me realize how misguided we are in our opinions on race and colored people in general."

Barbara sighed, "I hope Liz realizes the same and stops her racist ranting forever."

It was nearly 4:00 AM, and the house was tranquil. Arun was only half asleep, in case Liz woke up. Chris was fast asleep. All the health-markers were reassuring, and there was no reason for concern. Arun tried to doze off once more. However, in about a few minutes, he heard a slight murmur from Liz, so he got up and went to her. The maid also woke up and went to call the Howards.

Liz opened her eyes and said, "Where am I?"

Barbara and Jeff came up to her, and Barbara replied, "You are on your bed in our house, and the time is five minutes past four in the morning. We are so happy to hear from you speak. We were so worried."

Arun asked them to let Liz do the talking. He did not want her to suffer unnecessary emotional stress by bringing up the accident and her injuries. They apologized to him and promised to allow only Liz to talk.

Liz looked at him, puzzled. "Why are you here? How did you get in, and who let you in?" Barbara said, "Please calm down. You had an accident and hit a tree. You were badly injured, and Chris in concussion. However, she recovered and was able to talk to dad and me last night. Arun is a medical doctor – he was at the scene of the accident, brought you here, and has been taking exceptional care of you both."

Liz was not pleased to hear that the nigger was a doctor responsible for her rescue. She felt that she would rather be dead than be cared for by this colored doctor. She also knew that she had to put up with it for now and hoped she would never see him again and would not have to call on his services even if he was the only doctor left in this world.

He was about to ask her whether she wanted some soup and bread but changed his mind when he saw the look on her face, and he wisely left it to the maid to ask about any food she needed.

Arun said, "Miss Howard, I'm going to remove the tubes and sensors so that you can sit upright. After your meal, I will have to put them back to monitor your pulse and BP. I know you are very annoyed to see me here and might even be wishing me gone. I will oblige you on that once you start walking again tomorrow. But, for the moment, you have no option but to have me around. For now, if you have pain anywhere or headaches, let me know at once. Please do not let your opinion about me interfere with my professional help to you and your sister for the next few hours."

He gently removed the tubes and sensors and adjusted the pillows so that she could sit upright. Liz looked at her and dress and scowled. "Did you change my dress and peep at a white girl's body? How deprived are you?"

Before Barbara could intervene, Arun laughed and said, "Miss Howard, you were unconscious and just a body to me medically. Yours is not the first one I have seen, and it won't be the last. That privilege comes with the medical profession."

Barbara saw Liz flush and quickly intervened, "Liz, darling, the maid did that on his instructions, and he left the room when you were undressed. He was just teasing you."

Arun could sense the bitterness and anger in her and the tension in the room. Barbara and Jeff were equally tense and looked at Arun with a feeling of guilt. He left the room without looking at Liz. They all noticed his action and felt very sorry for him. Barbara did not want to admonish Liz when she was in bed and was hurting.

Liz was very angry at Arun's remarks, but she was hungrier. She told the maid she would love the soup and bread. She asked her mum who the doctor was. Barbara said, "Darling Liz, I do not know anything other than that he is called Dr. Ayer, and he is the new GP in the village. We like him very much, and he has been taking good care of you both. More about all this tomorrow, when you feel better. Do try to be civil to him, darling."

Liz said, "Mum and Dad, I do not like him calling you by your first names; that shows how uncouth he is and reflects on his upbringing. It is these things that annoy me about him – and about colored people!"

Barbara said, "Oh Liz, he did address us as Mrs. and Mr. Howard. I told him to call us by our first names from now on. He was anything but rude, and there is nothing wrong with his upbringing. It's all about your perception. For now, please do not think of him if it annoys you; get some sleep, and we will talk tomorrow after you have rested."

Liz wanted more soup and bread with a meat dish, but Arun had told the maid not to give her any meat for 24 hours and even restrict eggs to two per day. Liz realized she had to put up with this doctor, and she should get quickly on her feet to be free of him.

When Barbara came to let Arun know that Liz was ready to sleep, he straightened the pillows and reconnected the sensors. Liz reacted with anger when he removed the top layer of clothing leaving her breasts visible, but that is what he had to do to connect the sensors to her chest. Arun ignored her anger and covered her with sheets again. He then positioned himself so that he could see the girls' faces and the monitors and then dozed off.

The next day was Sunday – a lovely sunny day with chirruping birds and bright sun filtering through the curtains. Arun got up when the clock chimed 7:00, checked that the readings were okay, and then started disconnecting the sensors from the meters. He told the maid to remove the connection to the bodies, and he would send someone soon to be with the girls. He then phoned Sandra and Debbie and requested them to come ASAP, which they agreed to do. He told them to do 6-hour shifts with Sandra starting first at 8:00 AM and Debra coming in at 2:00 PM to relieve her. When Sandra arrived, he briefly explained the events of the previous evening and night and said she could call him anytime if she were unsure. She only had to ensure that the girls rested and did not walk around unduly, for another 24 hours. Walking to the bathroom was the only exemption.

He told the maid that as the Howards were sleeping, he did not want to wake them, but that Sandra would take care of the girls till 2 PM and Debra from 2 to 8 PM. He thanked every maid, staff, the Head Chef, and a security guard for their help and left.

CHAPTER 7

Removing a few thorns from the flesh.

Arun drove back to the Surgery, tired and sleepy. He had taken the weekend off for doing several chores, but he decided to put off a lot due to the accident. Arun asked Dave and Sally to return to the Surgery but leaving the monitors and connectors. Arun thanked them for their help on a Saturday and said they would be paid double time with overtime. Arun remembered when asked by Barbara how much would he pay Dave and Sally to look after Liz and Chris; he said he would pay them double time with overtime. She had opened her purse and given Arun GBP 25 for each and said Arun should not bear any surgery costs for now, and she would pay for all the staff costs. Arun, jokingly, said that his services were for free.

Back at the Surgery, Arun dealt with a new problem that had cropped up. Arun had had some reservations about Dennis for a few weeks. He had observed Dennis and Mary trying to open the locked chest of drawers and filing cabinets several times. However, on Friday evening, when he saw them trying to open the locked filing cabinets, he had lost his cool.

"Dennis! Mary! Why are you trying to break into those locked drawers and cabinets?" he demanded.

"We were just looking to see if there were papers there that needed attention," Dennis said lamely.

"What sort of papers?"

"Anything to do with payments received or made."

"Payments? From whom?" Arun demanded sternly.

"No one in particular, but I had not seen any papers from the Health Authority to the surgery, and I wanted to process those."

"Right at the beginning, even before you started working here, I told you not to worry about the Surgery income. Those details are confidential, and I will process them in my own time. If I wanted you to do that, I would have given the details to you. Please do not ever open the locked chest of drawers or filing cabinets. Neither you nor Mary should ever enter my office for any papers, when I am not present. I hope I make myself clear to you both."

"I have never been spoken to like this ever before. I take offense at your tone of voice," Dennis bristled.

"I am sorry, I had to make those comments, and if you feel so very aggrieved, you should stop work as of now."

"We will think it over and let you know after the weekend, about continuing to work here."

Arun was keen to terminate the working relationship, even though they had useful contacts in the community. After the Surgery opened, in a month or so, he had built up his connections in the village, and the need for Mary and Dennis in this area was no longer crucial. He did not want to depend on anyone for anything, as it gave that person a slight edge. In their perception, they thought they were indispensable and could take liberties. He felt the decision to remove them from the Surgery would be beneficial in the long run. He began planning how to do it with minimal fuss.

After reaching Surgery, he had a shower and a light breakfast. He had asked Sally to take the weekend off, as he was planning to take care of cooking himself. He remembered telling her that he would be going

34

to the hospital for an ophthalmology clinic and would eat there. He then had a telephone call from Sandra around 10:00 AM

"Doctor, both the ladies are up. Chris is very cheerful and talkative. She had a hearty breakfast without meat and coffee in bed. She is reading the morning papers. Liz got up around the same time as Chris and demanded a full English breakfast of egg, sausage, bacon, and beans with toast and coffee. The maid, as advised, gave her two fried eggs, toast and beans followed by coffee. She got an earful from Liz. In that commotion, the lady of the house came and calmed Liz down and said it would be for just one more day and to please follow the Doctor's orders."

"How about the readings of pulse and BP for both?"

"For both: normal; For Chris: Pulse 75 and BP 120/70; for Liz: Pulse 80 and BP 120/75. Liz's cuts are healing, and I have put on some more ointment. I suggested a hot towel rub instead of a bath for both ladies, and they agreed."

"Have you had breakfast, and are you being taken care of?"

"Doctor,' Sandra laughed, "I am getting the royal treatment. I have never received such treatment before!"

"Good! Let me know if things change."

Arun decided to visit Dick and Cathy in the morning and seek some help to replace Mary and Dennis. The shop was quiet on Sundays apart from one or two customers who came in for the morning papers.

"Cathy and Dick, I need to talk to you about getting some more people to work in the surgery, and I need some advice," Arun said.

"Doctor, let's go into the next room and talk, while Cathy looks after the shop." Dick led the way to the adjacent room.

Arun briefly told him about the issues he had with Dennis and Mary and asked Dick to keep it confidential. He also said that he would like to replace them immediately, if possible.

"Hmm" Dick mused, "I have a couple, who may be right for you. Both are exceedingly polite and gentle and do not have any issues working with people of color. Stephen and Jessica King – they are Barbara Howard's parents. Jessica worked as a nurse, some years ago, and Stephen, as a retired insurance agent. They have lived in the village for over 40 years."

"What a surprise! The world gets smaller and smaller! When can I see them?"

Dick: "Usually, they go to Barbara's place for lunch on Sundays and are back by 6:00 PM."

Cathy, when told about the idea, offered to telephone them. "I will make the telephone call in a few minutes and let you both know the outcome."

Cathy left to make the call, and Arun and Dick sat down with their tea and biscuits. Cathy returned with a smile on her face.

"Jessica and Stephen are at home. They are happy to meet right away. I said I would call them back in a few minutes to confirm."

Arun was delighted and agreed to the meeting, and Dick accompanied him to their residence and made the introductions.

Stephen said, "We have heard a lot of good things about you and how you decided to settle for a smaller fortune in this small village, forgoing the big fortune you were making in London."

Arun countered, "I am surprised you know a lot about me, and I know nothing about you two, except that you are Barbara's parents."

After that, Arun got to the point and asked them whether they would be able to work for him in the Surgery.

"As for what?" Stephen asked. "We are keen to help as it is for the good of the village. What kind of work would we do, and when should we start?"

"Mrs. King can assist the main nurse – I have advertised for one. And Mr. King, you can help me with stock, orders, invoices, payments, petty cash and so on. I will handle all accounts dealing with revenue. If this is agreeable to you, you can start tomorrow morning, and we will discuss your pay and the hours of work."

Jessica said, "Doctor, you will have to lead me by hand till I get settled. Also, please call me Jessica and my husband, Stephen, from now on. We will always call you 'Doctor' in Surgery and on formal occasions."

"Please call me Arun on other occasions, and I am delighted to have you both on board."

Arun then bid them goodbye. He then returned to the Surgery and telephoned Dennis. Ten minutes later, Mary and Dennis were in his office.

"Well, Dennis, you wanted to say something… what about it?"

"Arun, Mary, and I feel that there's too much work in the Surgery, and it's getting stressful. I learnt on Saturday that I have diabetes, and I will be grateful if you undertake further investigation and advise me on what I should do."

"Dennis, diabetes strikes nearly 50-60% of the population and, with the right diet, exercise, and medication, one can live for a very long time. I will start the tests tomorrow. Please come at 8:00 AM before the other patients arrive."

"Thank you! It means that we will not be working in Surgery from tomorrow. I am sad it had to end this way, but income is not as important as health, and we both feel it's time to call it a day. We want to relax and take it easy. We are glad you came to the village to resurrect the Surgery, and we are happy about the part we played in it."

"Both of you supported me at the formative stage, and I will always be grateful to for that," Arun said cordially.

They left before mid-day, and Arun was glad that there was no unpleasantness. He went to the kitchen to make a simple meal when the doorbell rang. It was from Sally. She had cooked some pasta and stir-fry vegetables and decided to bring them around. He thanked her profusely and felt that this was one of those days when everything went well.

CHAPTER 8

Tables turned

Arun had his usual afternoon kip for 30 minutes. He decided to tidy his wardrobe, a job he had avoided for over five weeks. As he was about to begin, there was a telephone call. He answered, "Surgery."

Barbara asked, "Is that Arun?"

Barbara wanted him to come over to the house. She said the girls were doing fine, but being on Sunday, it was better to discuss a few things today as they were likely to be swamped tomorrow.

Arun: "Barbara, much as I would like to come, I think I should refuse because your elder daughter, Liz, does not like me. My presence will be very stressful her. Let her get better; our discussion can wait."

Barbara said, "Arun, please trust me. Liz also wanted this meeting today, as did Chris. Please do come and have dinner with us. The Head Chef, following Sally's instructions, will prepare special food for you. We would like you to come soon, preferably in the next 30 minutes, so that we all could have a long chat about the accident and the prognosis for the future."

"Okay, I will be there shortly."

Arun was not in a mood to have another argument with Liz, but at the same time felt he should hear their side of the story regarding the accident, and the girls should also know what had happened when he came upon that scene. He reached their house in 20 minutes and gave a bouquet, usually left in the surgery by Sally, to Barbara, as he did not want to go empty-handed, and, as a teetotaler, he did not have any wines in the Surgery to bring.

Barbara said, "Arun, you should not have bothered with flowers, but anyway, thank you for the wonderful selection. Let us go to the bedroom as the girls are sitting up and have a long chat. As the girls are feeling better, they told Sandra that no further medical supervision was needed, and she also agreed. So, Debbie will not be becoming. House is back to normal in one way but very special in another way, in that you have come."

"Thanks for the nice words about the flowers, but it was Sally's choosing. Glad Sandra was of help. She did tell me about the ladies not wanting Debbie for the afternoon. She will collect the monitors tomorrow and bring them to the surgery."

"Doctor, why are you referring to us as two ladies? Please call me Chris and my sister Liz from now on."

Arun smiled, "It is nice of you, Chris, to make that suggestion. I will not take the other one's permission to be taken for granted at this stage."

"Oh, Liz doesn't mind; do you, sis?"

Liz did not reply and turned her gaze elsewhere. Barbara and Jeff were embarrassed by her attitude, but they kept quiet.

Barbara said, "I do not know where to begin; do you have any idea, Arun?"

Arun nodded. "Yesterday I started telling you about our first meeting in the shop followed by the one in the café during lunch and then later, the accident. Each of you should also share your version of what happened so that we will have a balanced view."

Jeff said, "I agree it is the best way to start is from the beginning. So please, Chris, you start."

Chris narrated the incident at the shop and how taken aback they had been when Arun had accosted them regarding the items they had purchased quite innocently. "Liz got upset and called him a "nigger" for having the temerity to speak to us like that. I didn't like her language but didn't want to argue with her in public, so I held my peace," she shrugged.

"I felt sorry for him and admired how he took the racist comments on the chin, quite calmly.

We met him by chance, in the café yesterday and he sent us a letter of apology letter. It was a very politely worded. I have a note here. Liz wanted to tear it to pieces, but I salvaged it."

She showed the letter to her mum and then to her dad. They were equally impressed.

"The next time we saw him was when he was driving ahead of us in the lane. He moved to one side to let Liz pass as she was honking for nearly a mile. He could not find any passing spots earlier; otherwise, I'm sure he would have let her pass sooner. Liz once again made some racist remarks, and told him to go back to his country and ride bullock carts! He said he would do that soon. Liz then steamed off, and a mile or so later, Liz swerved when a lamb ran across the lane, but we ended up skidding off the road and hitting a tree. I don't remember anything after that till I woke up here."

"Chris, your narration tallies exactly with what Arun has told Jeff and me," Barbara said. "We now know how the accident happened. Liz, would you care to tell us your side of the story?"

Liz shrugged, "There's nothing to say beyond what Chris said – but, of course, my reactions are somewhat different. Chris was never in Botswana for any length of time, but I was. And I remember the rioting, the anarchy, and the constant fear of people of color. I've resented people of color ever since. No wonder his implied advice, pissed me off." She nodded disdainfully towards Arun. "At that moment, I thought he was a waste of space and would have liked to make him disappear for good. As for the shopkeeper apologizing on my behalf…. humph! I hated both the men," she replied in disgust. "Then, when we saw him in the café, what does he do but send us a letter, which received a lot of unwanted attention from the people around. A black man sent a letter to white girls and asked a waitress to deliver, who was anything but discreet in her manner! Do you blame me for not appreciating the apology?"

She drew a calming breath and continued, "Driving home, I was annoyed with the driver of the Austin car in front of me and thought it must be a very old man driving it like a snail. Only when he moved to the side to let me pass, did I realize it was the same person we had met in the shop and the café! I gave him a piece of my mind about going back to his country and driving bullock carts. His reply that he would do it soon only made me angrier. The cheek of him! He also gave me some formal advice about driving slowly in case of accidents – on roads I have driven on all my life! I'm sure he jinxed me. It must be his negative energy that drove me off the road!" she declared hotly.

"Now, Liz…" Barbara said in a friendly tone, "I don't know why you call him 'this person' while he calls you Miss Howard. Why don't you call each other by your first names as Chris does with Arun?"

"Well, I have no objection," Arun interjected, "but Miss Howard might feel it is too early to be on a first-name basis, and I will respect her judgment on that. No need to force the issue."

"I agree to decide on this issue later!" Liz said emphatically. "Why, I may not even want to see him after today. Once I can walk, I will see my GP in the next Town for advice."

Barbra, Jeff, and Chris disapproved of Liz's vehemence. They felt she was intent on insulting Arun. However, Arun seemed very calm and continued to smile as he had done the whole evening.

"A patient in the UK has the right to choose any GP as their principal physician," he said mildly. "So, it's entirely up to you."

He continued: "Now, regarding the accident: After you passed me, I was motoring along when I heard a loud noise ahead of me. At first, I thought some farmers were making a commotion with their equipment. However, as I turned a bend, I saw the accident. I immediately rushed over to check your condition. First, I switched off the engine and removed the ignition key. I could see blood on your forehead, Miss Howard, cuts around the nose and face and bruising on your right arm. Chris was unconscious but did not have any superficial cuts or bruises. I checked your pulses and found them to be high. I quickly pulled the back seats down in my car and transferred you both. I cleaned your wounds to stop the bleeding and put a tincture. I took the liberty of going through your bag, Miss Howard, and your driving license gave me your address. I also confirmed it by asking Chris, who was nearly unconscious. Luckily, your mother was in the garden and was made aware of the accident. The rest, you know."

He paused for a moment and then continued, "I must say your remarks about driving a bullock cart amused, rather than insulting me. I took it as a jest: it was a perfect analogy," he replied. "Incidentally, I'm not going to leave the country just because of an angry remark from a beautiful lady."

There were smiles on the faces of all four of them – more so on Liz's.

Chris: "I must thank you for being there for us, and I will always be grateful to you. Thank you for collecting the other valuables we left in the car – handbags, library books, shopping bags – our expensive purchases."

"Tell me one thing," Chris continued as Arun waved away her thanks. "That day in the shop? Why did not you tell us you were a doctor?"

"You know, Chris, in life, one has to respect people, as one sees them and not because they are famous, wealthy or possess power and influence in industry or politics. My profession commands instant respect. But by not declaring that I'm a doctor, I make sure that people convey their honest feelings – as Miss Howard did. Incidentally, none of her comments upset me, then or even now, honestly."

Chris said, "Do you know, Liz and I have applied for jobs at the surgery to a Dr. Ayer. Is that you?"

He nodded. "My surname was Iyer but I changed it to Ayer after coming to London."

"Now, what happens to my application? Do I still have a chance?" Chris asked eagerly.

Arun said, "None of this weekend's happenings has any bearing on your application. If your qualifications, experience, and willingness to commit to the surgery, matches my needs, then the job is yours. Incidentally, I noticed your names but did not go over your CV's in detail. Please give them to me now so that I can decide in a few minutes."

Chris got her CV and gave it to Arun. He told her to come with him to the other end of the large living room. He decided that though her experience as a nurse was minimal, with extensive training and enough guidance, she could prove to be an asset. In any case, she was the only applicant. He told her that she got the job and could start tomorrow.

Chris was extremely grateful to Arun, as she had given up hope of getting a career in the village and being close to her parents. In fact, in her excitement, she almost hugged him but drew back. She went back to her parents at the other end of the room

Arun: "Jeff and Barbara, I would like you to help me with the surgery work in areas suitable to you both. If you are agreeable, we can discuss this in the surgery tomorrow."

Barbara was delighted, "I would also like to volunteer my services. You have been like an angel to us, saving our girls, and taking good care of them. Jeff will also agree that we will help you as much as we can."

"Many thanks, Barbara. I'm sure we can work out timing that suits you," Arun said enthusiastically.

Jeff said, "Now it's 6:00 PM; we have talked for nearly four hours straight. I am glad we cleared the air. I hope, in time, Liz, too, will come around. She has such strong views on everything. I still don't understand why she hates colored people so much."

Arun said, "I have studied people in my profession – patients, doctors, staff… relationships between patients and others. I have analyzed them to know 'why they say, what they say' and 'why they do, what they do.' I don't jump to quick conclusions about a person's behavior or attitude. I try to avoid being critical of people.

I do appreciate Miss Howard's strength of character and her forthrightness. She doesn't mince her words. One will always know where they stand with her. I do not think she hates people; on the contrary, she is afraid to love people. She finds love involves considerable emotional feelings, which she does not want to share at this crucial period of her life."

Jeff sighed, "That is a very generous assessment. I only hope that Liz will have a change of heart at least with you, so she is more civil and respectful."

Barbara broke in, "Arun, please join us for dinner soon. The cooks are preparing special vegetarian food for you. We have two guests joining us for dinner, besides you and my parents, Stephen and Jessica King."

"I was introduced to them for a short period this morning, " Arun said quickly. He had not anticipated meeting them again so soon.

The doorbell rang, and Barbara's parents arrived. They were surprised to see Arun.

Barbara said, "Mum and Dad let me explain everything that has happened in the last two days," and took them into the next room.

Chris wanted to ask Arun some more about the surgery, and they went to another corner of the dining room, and Arun filled her in, till Barbara announced that it was time for dinner.

Arun found himself seated between Chris and Stephen, facing Liz, which she didn't like. She would have instead skipped dinner and gone to her room. Arun noticed her discomfort and felt sorry for her.

Stephen said that he and Jessica were glad that the Doctor comes to the rescue of his granddaughters.

Stephen said, "I told you Arun, you have come here to a small village to make a small fortune forgoing the big fortune you have been making in the big city of London. That's very decent of you. My friend, a medical consultant in BMA, spoke about you in glowing terms. That's why Jessica and I decided to work for you. Salary is not as important to us as being part of history being made in this village by you. Liz, I would request you to reconsider too and agree to work for this young man."

Arun quickly said, "Stephen, many thanks for your kind words. I have a lot of plans for this village. I would like the village people to be happy with me, as their GP, and with the surgery facilities. I will gather the right team together. I request you, please do not pressure Miss Howard to join me."

Liz hung her head, "I thank you, Doctor, for your kind words. I must confess that I'm intrigued by your analysis, and your attempt to judge me fairly in such a short time. It speaks volumes about your skills and abilities. I also found you calm, but sometimes too slow for my liking. I do not like to rush in and make decisions without analyzing people. I might even talk to you in private about what I should do. I am deeply sorry for all the offensive remarks I have made, and such thoughts will not cross my mind or heart ever again. I am sorry."

On hearing this, Barbara and the whole family were in tears and gave Liz a considerable hug, feeling that the prodigal daughter had returned safe and sound.

Barbara beamed, "I am speaking for all of us, Arun, that you have brought the biggest and most favorable change to our lives and brought our dear daughter, Liz, home to us. Liz, we are so happy with your change of heart. Don't ever look back!"

After dinner and coffee, Arun said goodbye. Chris suddenly gave him a big hug and a peck on his cheek in parting. Even he blushed!

CHAPTER 9

Humble beginnings

Arun was quite excited about the Surgery being staffed well, within one month, and he thought his work pressure would decrease soon. He had not found a Practice Manager or a Personal Assistant yet. He expected that these vacancies would be filled eventually or might even get filled quickly from unexpected sources.

On Monday morning, Arun got up as usual, at 5.30 AM, and he was ready for his daily duties, after a shower and breakfast by 7:00 AM. He went through his mail and saw that one of his friends, Alex Bailey, dissatisfied with his life in a city hospital, as an administrator, wanted to relocate and asked him to look out for any job opportunities for him near his area. He smiled and put it aside for future consideration. Arun's payment reports, from the Health Authority, was in a pile. He checked the amounts and then filed the reports immediately, opening the locked filing cabinet and then re-locking it. He then found the rest of the mail were bills from contractors for work done around the premises, and he put them in a separate pile to deal with later.

He took a look around the Surgery and found all the rooms were immaculately clean and up to medical standards. Dave had done a splendid job of renovating the Surgery and Sally had helped him with the daily cleaning, so that the dusty atmosphere, which had prevailed during the first four weeks, had been eradicated. Another two weeks of painting and furnishing meant that the Surgery was fully operational eight weeks after his arrival in the village. He had managed to see patients, from the third week itself, by moving from one room to another room as the work got completed.

At first, the patients had started coming in tiny numbers, about 6-10 per day for about a week; this then increased to 20-25 a day, and now there were about 35-40 patients a day. Wednesday was a half-day – morning till noon; Saturdays and Sundays, the Surgery was closed. He usually went to the nearby hospital for ophthalmology appointments on the off days.

He had never had a free day so far, but this did not bother him as he had no social life. No one had invited him to their homes, and the only people he had interacted with besides his patients, were the owners of corner stores, bank employees, estate agents, tradespeople, and the like. The Open Day held after six weeks had attracted a good crowd, including many who came out of sheer curiosity to see what the colored GP had been up to, though they had no intention of availing his services.

Arun also found that there was a group of 10-12 people who were hardcore racists and did not want a 'nigger' to be their GP. The fact that no white doctor had volunteered to serve in their community had not cleared their muddled thinking. Race feelings ran so high and were so ingrained in their lives. They even resorted to illegal acts to prevent such a person from working in the Village. Gradually Arun came to know that this racist group met clandestinely in a nearby small Town, late in the evenings, not to attract attention. They had a bodyguard to ensure that only members who supported their intents to maintain the racial purity of the Village were allowed in and no dissenters. Arun was advised not to drive using the small lane, as he could be cornered and assaulted. The Village police officer, who advised him on these measures, confessed that he was powerless to do much, as he had only one assistant. It was challenging to monitor the group as they kept changing meeting places every time. They met at least once a fortnight; more, if they felt action was imminent.

The police had put up posters around the surgery premises, parks and community centers, warning against vandalism, and malicious damage to property, particularly to the newly renovated Surgery. Notices stated that the perpetrators would be severely dealt with, which might involve fines and even long-term imprisonment. Two officers patrolled the village every night looking for any signs of nefarious activity. The villagers also formed a small vigilante committee to complement police efforts. The core group had their meetings under the pretext of fundraising for a children's charity in secret venues. The group of 12 had four female members and that the leader was a young lady.

This information was known to most of the villagers, but Arun only got to hear it by chance through Dave, about two days ago. It was not the core group's existence that worried him but the fact that it included four women. He wondered if Liz had been a part of the group. If so, in light of her change of heart the previous night, perhaps she could be persuaded to disband the group and dissuade them from further hostilities. He decided to talk to her and clarify these issues.

Arun hoped Liz would come to the Surgery sometime that week to discuss doing some work for him. Even though she had said she would, Arun felt that it was far from what she wanted to do. Maybe, Liz had just wanted to end the evening's discussions on a pleasant note so that Arun would leave. He had no real faith that she would ever want to meet him in private, and that too, work for him. It was too much to expect from such an antagonist. Perhaps it was better to leave things to evolve slowly; as it is, he had his plate full.

He had lots of plans for the village to expand the medical facilities, which would also create more job opportunities, and he needed everyone's support. But with news of the core group coming to light, he felt he had to be watchful and beware of Trojan Horse's gifts.

Arun then started to work out who would fit in where. The present two receptionists, Sandra and Debra, were terrific but he needed two more. Medical Secretary, Practice Manager, and nurse posts were still vacant. He had a part-time nurse in Jessica, for the time being, and when Chris started work, she would be the nurse position would be filled. Stephen could take over the administrative job relating to stores, stocks, and ancillary jobs. He still needed a Personal Assistant. He needed to find roles for Barbara and Jeff as well.

Chris came at 8:00 AM, as did Jessica. Arun showed them the nurse's consulting rooms and took them through the various equipment, procedure files, medical stock, and so on. He had made his first appointment at 9:30 AM to give him time to give his new staff a thorough briefing. Stephen was shown to his cabin and shown the filing cabinets. Barbara came at 9:00 AM, and she was happy to see Chris in uniform. Barbara was pleased to see Chris doing the work she loved and had trained. How she would like to see Liz do the same, she thought. Barbara wanted to work as a Secretary, taking care of the typing and filing. She offered to come in for four hours each day on Tuesdays, Wednesdays, and Thursdays. Arun felt that she could serve as a Medical Secretary for the time being.

At lunchtime, they all had a meeting in the small room used for lunch. Chris was very excited though she had only had to attend to simple cases of cold, flu, and some prenatal check-ups. Jessica had only had a few patients come in for health and diabetes checks.

Barbara had an in-tray full of material to type up, and she had completed half of it. She was hopeful of finishing it by the time she left at 2:00 PM. Stephen was on top of his work and had nothing to report. Arun was happy that the morning sessions went well.

The afternoon asthma clinic and the evening surgery also went smoothly. Then all the staff left, except for Chris. She said she wanted to talk to him for a few minutes.

Chris said, "Doctor, as mum says, you are like an Angel of Mercy to our family – saving both our lives. The mechanic said that if you had not switched off the ignition, the leaking fuel might have ignited and burnt the car." She shuddered at the thought.

"Thank you for those kind words. When did the mechanic tell you this?"

"Last night. He drove the car back after you left. All of us were stunned to hear what a near-miss we had and unanimously agreed that it was very sharp thinking of you to act so calmly in an emergency. We owe you so much. Even Liz said so."

"Hmm... change of heart, yeah? I did a course on accident

management, which covered these emergency procedures as well as patient care. So, your thanks should be to the course and its tutors."

"We all know you are very modest and make light of your achievements.

You are a hero in our eyes, and that is what I wanted to tell you," Chris said, looking at him with shiny eyes.

"Chris," Arun said firmly, "stop building me up into some kind of superhero. I did what any human being would do, just lucky to be there at that time. Let's not refer to this issue anymore. Promise me that you'll tell the others as well."

"I will tell them, and I cannot promise that they will not bring it up."

She was about to leave and asked if there was anything further to discuss. Arun requested her to come with him, and they went into the back garden. Dave and Sally were near a flowerbed considering what plants to put in and whether a small water fountain with a rock garden would be suitable.

Arun said, "Please do whatever you both want, but I would like to have some accommodation built here with three rooms, each room with an ensuite bathroom and a kitchen."

Dave said, "If you don't mind my asking, what is the purpose of this accommodation?"

"I'd like to see my Wednesday ophthalmology patients here, rather than at the hospital, and after treatment, they need a place to recuperate for a night."

Dave mulled it over. "Doctor, please wait for a few days. There may be a house nearby coming up for sale which can be purchased and modified for the purpose,"

"Dave, I am indebted to you for this information. I can wait a few weeks to know about the availability of a house. Thank you, Sally and Chris, for your time."

Sally said, "Doctor, I have to go out this evening, and I did not cook your food. You will have to manage tonight's dinner on your own. I'm sorry."

"I have a great idea!" Chris said, with her usual enthusiasm. "Why don't I send you dinner from the house so that you can spend your time on other medical issues."

Arun smiled, "Many thanks, Chris. Sometimes getting away from medical issues is good therapy; don't worry, I'll manage."

Then they dispersed. Chris returned home, and so did Dave, but Sally stayed on for a few more minutes.

Arun turned to her "I have a lot of household chores to do like sorting out papers, drawers, filing cabinet, laundry, ironing, and general dusting and tidying. Sally, can you also take these on? I will reimburse you, of course. Will an additional GBP 15 cover it?"

"Certainly, I will take over the household chores from tomorrow. I am very grateful to you for being so kind to Dave and me. Thank you!" She hugged him and pecked his cheek.

Her gratitude touched Arun and much relieved that he had successfully delegated his never-ending chores.

CHAPTER 10

Resurrection

The next day's surgery was uneventful. The staff was settling well, helped by the fact that the patient influx was still low, so they had time to learn their jobs. The Village had not yet got used to the new GP and the facilities offered. Many overcame their initial resistance to his color, as they found him pleasant and very helpful, compared to the cantankerous GP they had a few years ago. The previous GP had alienated many people with his arrogance, and many had started treating themselves at home with herbs or alternative home remedies rather than seek his professional services. Sometimes, these alternatives did not work, and only then did they come to see the GP; many times, complications would have already set in.

Arun constantly reiterated that patients should come and see him at the first sign of symptoms, but he also knew that the change would take time and any amount of advice, or issuing leaflets about what to do and what not to do, would not speed up the process.

When they all sat down during lunch break, Chris said, "Doctor, as you are free this Wednesday, can you please come over to our house, as we have a few things to discuss?"

"I have no problem with discussing anything, but since four of your family are here, let's have our discussion hereafter surgery closes."

"Umm... the fact is, it's Liz who wants to talk with you."

"Well, if Liz wants to talk to me, she can pick up the phone. Or, she can come here in person."

"I agree," Barbara nodded. "Chris, Liz is a grown-up, independent lady who can speak for herself and not expect you to be her mouthpiece."

"Is it settled that tomorrow afternoon we have a discussion session here?"

Chris said, "I will confirm it tomorrow if that's all right with you, doctor."

"It is fine with me."

That evening, Arun went to meet Mr. Sanders, the newsagent, and the general store owner.

"Dick, I need a huge favor. I'd like to have all children below the age of 12 and those between13 to 25, both boys and girls. Is it possible to meet all of them in the park or the back garden of the Surgery? I will make sure Dave erects a marquee and, if I know the numbers, Sally will arrange snacks and cold drinks. What do you think? Can we swing a meeting from say from 10:00 AM to 12 noon?"

"I will put out feelers and let you know by the end of the week. The bank holiday weekend is in two weeks and, usually, we have a huge gathering in the park that day. Everyone shares duties with food and drinks. The Village committee usually bears the costs, so there is no need for the Surgery garden and for Sally to prepare sandwiches."

"That's even better!" Arun beamed. "If you can arrange a 2-hour session on that day, I'm happy to contribute to the committee. Whom should I contact for that?"

"You know him, and he works with you in the surgery," Dick laughed. "I'm talking of Stephen, Barbara's dad. He is very influential and popular with the villagers, and not just for his wealth. All the villagers respect him and will listen to him."

"Many thanks to you. Please let me know when you get further details."

Arun's mind was working overtime. He was surprised to hear about Stephen's influence in the Village. He wanted to talk to Stephen at once, but he calmed himself and felt that he should wait for an opportune time to talk about his plans and the need to have the younger generation attend the meeting.

The next day was a half-day, and after everyone had left by 12:30 PM, Arun received a phone call.

"Hello, it is the surgery... Dr. Ayer here. How may I help you?"

"This is Liz here. I would like to come in now and talk to you about a few things. Is this a good time?"

"It is a convenient time. Please do come. Will you join me for a light lunch as well? I am about to have some."

"I will. See you in ten minutes."

"Sally, there is going to be a guest. Please rustle up some lunch for her; she is due in ten minutes."

Sally hid a smile; she knew he was excited about his visitor.

"And Sally, please don't talk to anyone about the person who is coming to visit now. This visit is confidential for the time being."

"Oh, don't worry, I will set the dishes on the table and leave. That way, I will not see the person and not be tempted to talk about it."

Sally left shortly, well before the doorbell rang.

"Miss Howard," Arun ushered her inside. "Should we have lunch straight away or should I show you around first... that is if you would like a tour of the premises?"

"Lunch first, if you do not mind, doctor," Liz smiled.

He led her to the kitchen, and they sat down at the places set by Sally. Lunch was simple, consisting of stir-fried vegetables and a cheese omelet with only water; no wine. An apple with cheese was dessert.

"How basic one can get!" Liz thought.

Then Arun showed the consulting rooms, the ophthalmology clinic, the offices for the staff, the reception, waiting rooms, and so on, finishing up by the door to the first floor.

"What is behind that door?" Liz asked.

"It leads to two identical large flats; a large bedroom, ensuite bathroom, an office cum lounge, and a storeroom; then a WC and a common lounge. One apartment is mine. The other is for my assistant."

They then returned to the ground floor to his consulting room, ready to talk.

Liz went first: "I have a lot to get off my chest as I have been bottling it up ever since our first meeting in the shop. For some days, if there was a restless person in our house, it was none other than me!

I always felt separate from the rest of my family because of my attitude and thinking that no one understood me, and you got to the crux of the psychological issues confronting me. I had lost a lot of ground and respect from the family – all because of my attitude towards you.

I was angry with you in the shop because I assumed you were accusing me unfairly. I did not want to use the words colored and nigger, but they leaped to my lips, too late to retract them. I had never apologized to anyone, particularly to a 'nigger.' But even then, I thought you were different – you looked very erudite and gentlemanly, and also very handsome," she smiled.

Arun smiled and asked her to continue.

"When I met you again in the café, I was, for some inexplicable reason, quite pleased. But all that changed when you sent me a letter through the waitress. It was quite embarrassing for me. As most of the folks in the village do not look kindly on a man of color, sending a note to two white girls in front of everyone in the café. I felt the best thing I could do was to ignore the letter, even though it was well-meant." She looked at him directly and continued, "It takes a very generous heart to behave so gentlemanly after this and not to let it affect our future relationship; this will not come naturally to a lot of people. You must be a very thoughtful person looking to the future with a great deal of hope. You do not get flustered by racist comments even when they were downright insulting. But you behaved impeccably."

Arun said to her, "I am surprised there were so many sentiments at work in our encounter. It was also thoughtless of me to send that letter without considering your standing in the community. At that moment, I thought you both had passed through the small Town and were not residents in this area. However, that is no excuse – and I apologize for acting spontaneously without thinking it through. But please continue."

Liz sighed, "As for the accident, you did warn me about driving at high speed, but I felt that you were mocking me and laughing behind my back, and that drove me wild. My infamous temper took over, and logic and reason went out of the window."

"Miss Howard, you have now analyzed your actions and mine clearly and candidly. I must admit that my sarcastic acknowledgment may have been a tad unfair. I'm sorry if I've been insensitive."

Liz shook her head, " The fault is all mine. You know, ever since I was young, I was labeled as the one who was a racist and hated people of color. Every time I tried to break out of it, my family members would always remind me of my previous comments and provoke me by reiterating my sentiments. It was a losing battle. They did not realize how it affected me and may not believe it, but the effect on me was phenomenal and disastrous.

But you with your psychological insight showed that you understood me and shook me from the deep slumber I was in and forced me to re-examine myself. I was motivated to shake off the cloak of 'racist' and fight against it. I decided to fight against being labeled, from that day onwards, and I must thank you – not only saving my life and that of Chris' but giving me a chance to redeem myself. For that, I am eternally indebted to you."

"Miss Howard, you are very kind, and your sentiments touch me; more importantly, by you want to fight the stigma. I commend you for that."

"Doctor, will you please call me Liz from now on and not Miss Howard?"

"I will do so, and you call me Arun – except when we are in a professional work environment when you must call me 'doctor'?"

"I will observe the protocols nicely, doctor!"

"It is nearly two hours since you came. I am dying for my coffee made the South Indian way. Would you like to try some, Liz?"

"I would love to."

Arun then made two cups of coffee and brought it to her along with some biscuits. The stainless-steel coffee containers were small, and she had never seen them before. The taste of the coffee she found to be very exotic.

"Doctor, you mentioned my working for you. Much as I would like to, I feel I should not."

"Why? What are you afraid of?"

"I will be with all my family 24/7! I certainly want to be doing something separate from all of them. I don't think that will be possible in this surgery."

"If you had to do a job that does not involve any of them, will you be interested?"

"Most certainly. Is there such a job?"

"Yes, there is. I must explain that there are two types of jobs under the roof of this Surgery. I am a GP paid by the NHS, and so are all the staff who belong to the Surgery practice. Besides, I do private work in ophthalmology at a hospital on Wednesday afternoons, Saturdays, and Sundays. The NHS HQ knows this and allows me to do this, but it accounts for the Private income I generate. All accounts, expenditure, staff, are separate. None of the staff here will be involved in my private practice. Only my PA (personal assistant) will know all that. That PA has to be with me on all the three days in the hospital, act as a chauffeur, and also work discreetly in a separate office here in the Surgery. All details of my Private work should be kept confidential from the Surgery staff."

Liz: asked, "Are you asking to be your PA?"

"Why not? You will come to know more about the nature of my work, deal with the hospital, keep tabs on all appointments, travel, and food arrangements. Because of the late hours, the PA will have an apartment in the Surgery. The salary package will be generous and paid by me, but you will not be on the NHS payroll. Private health cover and pension provisions are part of the salary package. It's like operating an office within an office. Are you interested?"

"I am very nervous as I know nothing about hospitals and ophthalmology!"

"That's nothing to worry about as I will be with you and train you. You will also be given training at the hospital in certain areas of administration from time to time."

"Sounds good. When do you want me to start?"

"From tomorrow. And we will get the letter of appointment typed up. I hope you can do some typing and filing?"

"These are within my capabilities. Office management, I am comfortable with."

Arun said, "I know you have your family working here in the surgery. But please treat your role as confidential. You can say in general terms, for instance, that we had five operations, etc., but do not give outpatient details or outcomes of operations. All income details are also confidential. Any break in confidentiality and the PA will lose the job immediately. This condition has to be understood."

"I will not break your confidence and do my best to earn your respect by doing my duties well."

Liz rose to her feet. "I will see you tomorrow."

"Please come at 8:00 AM, before the others arrive so that I can brief you in detail. And Liz, don't come to the Surgery in an expensive sports car. Use a workhorse like a Mini, for coming to work."

"Message understood. I am happy that I came here and got a job that keeps me separate from the other members of my family. I am very thankful to you, Arun."

At that time, a telephone call came, and Arun was surprised to hear Barbara on the line. She wanted him for dinner, and there was to be no excuse. He just had to agree to that compelling invitation. He told Liz about the dinner at her place, and she was quite happy about it

Just as she was leaving, she suddenly hugged him and kissed him on both his cheeks. Arun asked why she was spoiling the day. She laughed and said that those were because he saved her life, and she did not want to do it in front of all her family as Chris had done.

Liz left for home satisfied and have achieved a lot of things which she never thought she would. She had won her first fight against the stigma of being labeled a racist.

CHAPTER 11

Psychology of Mind and Behavior

Arun got into his car and followed Liz to the house. The whole family including Steven, and Jessica, were waiting for them.

"I will give you all the news once we sit down in the lounge; all of what happened this afternoon, with 'blow by blow' details' – if you are not too bored to listen!" Liz declared with her usual dramatics.

"Bored? You must be joking! We are dying to know all the nitty-gritty of what transpired," Chris laughed.

Liz said that she spoke to Arun for over an hour, touching on her personal feelings and how she was trying to get out of the 'slot' of being a 'hater of colored people.'

Liz said, "I tried to change, but 'saying this and saying that' put me down. You all had a set opinion of me, which I could never shake off."

Barbara said, "I'm sure, none of us realized the bad effect we were having on you, very inadvertently. If only you had opened your heart and thoughts to us earlier, darling."

"Oh, I'm not saying that it was all your fault or anyone else's. The main fault lay with me, of course. For a grown girl, I should have known better. Anyway, let me tell you about what happened when I went to the Surgery this afternoon."

They were all pleasantly surprised that she had taken the initiative to clear the air with Arun. Not only that, but she had also got an excellent job as his PA. It was all moving too fast for them to comprehend.

Chris teased, "When did you graduate to calling him Arun from 'that person'?"

"Before he made the job offer!"

Everyone laughed.

"Liz, I'm detecting that you have a soft corner for Arun. Am I right?" Chris teased.

Liz said hotly, "This is about me and my hateful attitudes and remarks. That is what I wanted to talk about, and I have done it. Now I have to behave following that dictum. Do not deduce a relationship between us from issues like these."

"Hmm…" Chris said, not sounding the least convinced. "I will remember not to rush to conclusions, sis."

Jeff said, "So Arun, what does this PA role involve?"

"The PA role involves the 'A-Zee' of my Private work. I do ophthalmology operations and clinics in the hospital for two-and-half-days every week. The payments for such surgeries are quite high and many times more than my income from NHS GP surgery work. Stephen, you are right, I have taken a cut of several thousand GBP by coming here. At that time, I felt I had to give back to society, and that money is not everything."

Chris countered, "Arun, do you mean to say money is the root of all evil as the Good Book says?"

Arun smiled, "On the contrary, one needs money. The parable of the Good Samaritan implies the Good Samaritan was not poor. He had to be rich to help the poor. Also, I don't think the Good Book says, 'money is the root of all evil.' It is the improper pursuit of money that is 'root of all evil.' If one wants to help society, there is nothing wrong with having sufficient wealth to do so."

Barbara intervened, "Arun, you were telling us about the PA's role."

Arun detailed all that the role would involve and the timings Liz

60

would have to keep. "There is an apartment in the surgery, similar to mine, which Liz can occupy if she chooses to."

"You seem to have thought of everything," Stephen commented.

They spoke for a while, and then the topic reverts to Liz's change of attitude.

"Liz's explanation reminds me of an anecdote," Arun said. "There was a big order of live frogs for export from Madras to New York. The US firm sent a specialist expert to ensure that the frogs were packed carefully for the 12-hour journey. Workers were packing the frogs in a factory in Madras who had no formal education but were streetwise and full of wisdom gained from experience.

The frogs put in large 4-foot diameter caskets, with few bamboo prongs sticking out, to put the next box on top. The prongs created a gap of three inches so that air could circulate. But the company expert was very annoyed that the workers so ignorant that they could not comprehend that the frogs could easily escape through the three-inch gap?

He rudely accosted one of the local workers and asked him this query, but the man just laughed and said that this would not be the case with Indian frogs, perhaps with American frogs, but never Indian! The expert got angry about being ridiculed. 'What's so special about Indian frogs?' he sneered. The worker said that in the case of Indian frogs if one tried to jump out, three other frogs would pull it down and stop it moving out of the casket. It happened in business and all walks of life. He should understand Indian culture more before getting angry and being rude to people.

Many times, we all behave like the other three frogs. I am sure anytime Liz wanted to be rid of the racist tag, and she did not want any reference to her past remarks about these people. That sort of reminder was akin to pulling the jumping frog down. I am sure it happens in all families. Even for simple things like food – a family would have reminded a member that, 'you've never liked this or that' and prevented the person from wanting to try those items."

"I was in that situation of the jumping frog," Liz said. "You all loved me dearly, but you also boxed me in on this issue unknowingly. When Arun said those words the first time – about me being a nice person – it was a revelation. I felt very motivated to change from being a hater. I sincerely hope this new job will put me on the right path and move on from the past."

The above discussions led to psychology and behavior.

"In non-verbal communication, the term emotional intelligence refers to your ability to understand both your own emotions and those of other people. They play an important role in your relationships and professional life," Arun said that he would talk more about this in Surgery.

Barbara asked, "How does this affect us and our jobs?"

"We all have to understand patients and not pre-judge them and put them into slots – moaners, grumblers, etc. You must respect all patients and listen patiently to their complaints or criticisms. Always have a smiling face at all times".

The maid came and announced that the dinner was ready to be served, and it was a timely interlude. They went to the dining room and enjoyed a wonderful dinner. After coffee, Arun returned to the surgery.

There were no pecks on the cheeks for him tonight, and he did not expect any. The others did not know that Liz had pecked him on his cheeks in the surgery. He fondly thought of that as he left.

CHAPTER 12

The New Dawn

The next day dawned sunny and warm for the time of the year. Liz came early, as agreed, and Arun took her to her office, which was next to his consulting room. He organized it like that so his PA could keep tabs on him and remind him of his hospital appointments.

It was a large office with a circular table for meetings. The office had a sink, kettle, and coffee and tea-making facilities. Other snacks like sandwiches, one had to go to the kitchen, and in the dining room near the kitchen: only coffee, tea, and soft drinks in the offices excluding biscuits and chocolates should not be eaten in the consulting rooms or offices for health, safety, and hygiene issues. There were two filing cabinets with folders, and Liz had to slowly build up the files from the few, already in them, and keep the filing cabinets locked at all times. There was also a wooden cabinet for storing books, folders, and stationery. Liz was delighted with her domain. She put a picture of her family on the table to give it a personal touch.

Arun told her, "Liz, I am rescheduling two appointments in the afternoon clinic today to give us time to go to the hospital and introduce you to several key people you need to interact with frequently. Some consultants might be absent today, but they will be present during weekends. I told you last evening that I work all weekend and I would like my PA to drive me to the hospital and back. You may have some prior engagements, so please let me know whether you can make it this weekend."

"I'm free this weekend, but not so sure about the others. How about if I will let you know at the beginning of each week. Will that work?"

"That's fine by me. Why don't you take two days off during weekdays, if you're working weekends? I would prefer you to take two dis-continuous days like Tuesdays and Thursdays. What do you think?"

Liz agreed, " I will come to work for the whole of this week and take the days 'off' from the following week. I hope I will have an idea of the job to some extent by then."

"That's fine with me. Take down these telephone numbers and addresses – these are the key people you will interact with frequently. Also, please read this book on basic ophthalmology. It will give you an overview of the kind of cases that will come up. Incidentally, I am not disturbed during surgery or clinic hours, and unless the roof falls, other things will have to wait. You can send a note through the receptionists, and, even then, I may not respond immediately."

"Message understood, doctor. I will get to work as soon as I have finished my coffee."

The morning sessions went very quickly, and Liz was busy setting up the filing. Arun had said she would have to drive him to the hospital, a distance of 12 miles, which might take about 30 minutes. Following the accident, her car had been a write-off. She wondered if she could borrow Chris's car.

During lunch, Arun mentioned going to the hospital with Liz. He suggested that she drive his car, which came as a relief to her. He said that they should be back by 3:30 PM for the evening surgery.

Liz and Arun left at 1:00 PM in his car, an Austin Maxi estate. Liz drove very carefully, sticking to the speed limit. It was the first time she was driving after the accident.

Liz smiled, "Arun, you did not ask me whether I had driven after the accident and whether I am ready to drive!"

Arun said ruefully, "You are right, Liz. I forgot. I should have checked with you first. Do you want me to take over and drive?"

Liz nodded in the negative and went on, "Arun, in between filing,

I snatched some time to glance through the book on ophthalmology. It seems so intricate. You must have very steady hands and a keen eye to perform these surgeries."

"You're right – steady hands are a must. That's why I avoid strenuous physical work involving my hands lest I injure my fingers. A cut in the thumb or a sprain will affect my ability to hold the scissors and scalpel. Therefore, I rarely do work like pruning in the garden, working near rose plants, etc. It may sound overly cautious, but my patient's well-being depends on my fingers being in the best condition, so I prefer to pay tradesmen instead."

Arun continued, "By the way, I have brought my Leica automatic camera. I wanted to take a photo of you with the staff. I am sure all the male members of staff would like to have a photo with you. I am also sure that the other medics will envy me for my stunningly attractive PA!"

They smiled at each other and but did not say anymore as they pulled up outside the hospital entrance. The staff was waiting for their arrival. It's true to say they were stunned by Liz's beauty, and they were all smiles and keen to help her. Arun thought that all this fawning attention must be embarrassing for Liz – but would be suitable for his business.

The consultant took her into his office, and they all followed. In the meeting, they introduced themselves to Liz, and Arun suggested a photo of all of them so that Liz could remember their faces back in her office. They agreed immediately, and Arun took a few shots from various angles. The consultant gave her a short brief about the hospital, the Ophthalmology Department, and the people Liz had to liaise with regarding Dr. Ayer's patients. He stressed that the hospital did not have any other surgeon as skilled as Dr. Ayer and that they were very fortunate to have him there and gain experience by watching him operate. She had a separate room to use on the days she came in with the doctor and also a private place to sleep in, in case she had to stay over.

Liz was impressed with all the attention she was getting and gathered flirtatious glances from a couple of young doctors. She had not had much previous opportunity to meet so many young people of her age, which was an exhilarating experience for her. She glanced at Arun to see if he was jealous of the attention paid to her, particularly by the young medics. He seemed to be unmoved. She reminded herself that they hardly knew each other well enough to harbor strong romantic feelings; it was too soon to expect something. As she realized this, she felt a tinge of disappointment; she wanted Arun to be jealous.

Liz met all the relevant people and talked to them during the tea break. She collected handouts for reading and tried to absorb the medical jargon. She also took a copy of the appointments already scheduled for the next four-week period. Then they left for the village.

Arun asked, "Hmm... what did you think of the reception you got and the overall visit?"

"I enjoyed it and was overwhelmed. I am used to getting such attention in a social gathering, but this is my first time in a professional group."

"Did you enjoy flirting with the young medics?" Arun teased.

"I thought you didn't notice – or were you just pretending like it's beneath you to notice such trivia? Yes, I noticed their attention, but it didn't make me uncomfortable. I have to come to terms with an issue bothering me inside, and it may take months or years to sort out. I did find the visit very useful and the people helpful. The handouts were quite informative, and now I have to put my head down and try to understand and appreciate this medical area of human ailment."

"I am delighted to hear that you enjoyed the visit and found it useful. I also hope that, in time, you will come to terms with the issue that is bothering you. If there is any way I can help, please do not hesitate to ask me."

"The issue is too close to me. I need some solitude to clear my head. Now, let's talk about something else."

After a pause, Arun said, "Regarding this weekend's visits to the hospital, please let me know about your availability. I can understand if you have already made other engagements."

"Arun, I already told you I was available. As your PA, I will not make any other engagements as long as I am in your employ. Since you said last night that the job is for life, as long as I do not make any mistakes, I will always come with you."

"You are not have me on, are you?"

"Oh, for what?"

Arun said, "I suggest you take the rest of the afternoon off as you are near the Surgery. If necessary, even take tomorrow off. I liked you as were until yesterday, even when you were on the first day we met. It was better than the docile creature I see now."

"Chicken! I am not taking time off at your discretion. I am going to stay on until we close for the day. You will just have to put up with me as I am."

"Oh! What have I got myself into?"

You are safe, Dr. Ayer. I am not a monster, and I am not going to gobble you up."

Arun changed the subject, "Liz, if you do like, you can use this car to drive around – going home, to the shops, whatever. I am fine with you driving me to the hospital. I do not need the car otherwise. By next week the other car will come – an Austin Mini Estate, and you can have the sole use of that car as my PA. It's part of the salary package."

"Arun, you are amazing! I look forward to my Mini Estate next week. Mega, thanks."

They both smiled for different reasons; he at her flirting and she at his shyness around women. She touched his hands and squeezed them, and then blew a kiss. Arun was surprised and felt very shy.

They went to their respective rooms, and she began unloading books, pamphlets, and other leaflets onto her table and started to put them away neatly in various designated places for her to access. She then went to the kitchen, where she found Sally.

"Sally, are you very busy?"

"Yes, Miss Howard. I'm cooking an evening meal for the doctor."

"Sally, please call me Liz from now on. I have not told anyone else yet, and I do not want you to tell anyone. I will tell the doctor in the evening. I want it to be a surprise."

"What is it, Liz? My secrecy, I promise!"

"I will be moving into the apartment here from tomorrow. So, I would like you to cook for me as well. The doctor will sort out any payment due to you for this extra work."

Sally beamed, "I am so happy, Liz. The doctor is so lonely, and for

V S Mani

such a nice gentleman, you're joining as his PA is a Godsend. I will do the cooking for you if we agree to a menu each morning for the day. The doctor is a strict vegetarian and very particular, even about the oil and butter used. His menus are straightforward – stir-fried vegetables, lightly salted and spiced, usually with green chilies."

"Hmm…seems simple enough. For now, why don't you just double the quantity so that I have the same menu? I feel like becoming a vegetarian. Let's see how I like it. Is that okay with you, Sally?"

"As you say, Liz. I am happy to do it. The thought that you will be here from tomorrow puts a spring in my step."

"Calm down Sally, or someone may want to find out why you are so happy, and you may blurt out the message."

Sally said, "I will not say anything. I am hoping for a long association with you both and will not foul it up at the very start. Liz, please take good care of him, he has a heart of gold but does not open up easily, as if there is a dark secret lurking inside. You are clever enough to figure it out and keep him happy."

"Hmm, I didn't realize you were so observant. I will do my best and thank you for all your help."

Liz then went to her room. When the appointments finished at 6:00 PM, Arun came to see how she was getting on. Liz briefed him on her progress with the files, folders, cabinets, etc., without any mention of her talk with Sally. She then said she would see him in the morning and left with Chris.

Arun then went to his room – to deal with a load of paperwork waiting there. He liked to finish the day's work on the same day and did not wish to leave it to complete for a later time. That way, the letters were ready for Jessica to type as soon as she got in. He also checked the stocks and left a note to Stephen to order replacements in the morning from their established suppliers. Arun had allocated a room downstairs for a pharmacist so that the patients could leave their prescriptions and collect the medicines later, from the Surgery pharmacy itself. The local chemist, Mr. Stewart Atkins, was getting old, and he could not find anyone to take over the shop. Arun had spoken to Mr. Atkins about relocating his

68

pharmacy to the pharmacy room in his practice. Perhaps Dick could find someone to manage the shop.

Sally came up to him and said, "Doctor, Barbara told me that you would be having dinner with them at 7:00 PM, so I have not done any cooking for this evening. I hope that's all right."

"Sure. I will be there by 7:00 PM. Thank you very much. Have a nice evening, Sally."

CHAPTER 13

Mixed Interchanges

When Arun arrived at their house, all six family members were eagerly awaiting his arrival and to hear the latest news about the hospital visit that afternoon. They went into the kitchen, and the maid brought out the soft drinks. She knew by now the doctor was not one for alcohol – except for a few sips of wine on special occasions.

Liz then narrated everything that had happened from the time they had left the surgery to the time they left the hospital. Her family was impressed with the reception she had, the photo taken with them, and how they reacted to her beauty.

Chris asked, "Did you meet any handsome young consultants of our age there?"

"There were at least two good-looking, flirty consultants in that group."

Chris teased, "You mean even more charming than our doctor?"

Liz snapped, "Do you have any other questions?" She was embarrassed by her sister and planned to 'tell her off' privately.

Barbara: asked, "Were the matron and the senior consultant helpful, and did they offer you any training?"

"They gave me a training schedule and all the related books on ophthalmology: basics, leaflets, and clinic booking for four weeks starting from next week. A separate room to sleep in, if I ever had to stay overnight due to Arun's operations."

"Lucky you, sis! I am very envious of you. Tell us more so I can turn greener with envy."

"The consultant said they were lucky to have a surgeon like Arun and how they all benefitted from watching his operations and learning the various complex procedures. He is treated like a great celebrity there, commanding a lot of reverence and respect."

Chris said, "That's nice to know. But tell me more about the good-looking consultants."

"They tried to flirt with me, but I ignored them. I stood near Arun and held his hand to discourage them from approaching further. They took the hint and kept their distance. Arun did caution me before reaching the hospital that my appearance would turn most men on and that they would nudge to be near me and take pictures. Arun wanted me to take a picture with all the people so that I can remember who's who in the hospital. Many wanted their picture with me, but Arun did not give them his camera, and the hospital consultant ruled it was not a social party for taking pictures. He told the other consultants to behave themselves. They were very muted after that."

Chris pleaded, "Oh, Arun, will you let me loose with them if I came with you one weekend?"

"I am not sure. Do I have your parents' permission to turn you free?"

Barbara laughed, "Arun, please ignore her. Carry on, Liz."

Liz continued, "On the way back, we talked a lot. Arun told me that I could drive his Maxi Estate until I get my Mini Estate next week. That car is part of my perks for the job. I am very excited about it and told him so."

"Only just told him, Hmm, you could have done better than that, sis."

Barbara said firmly, "I do not like these innuendos between you two, not in front of us, and not in front of Arun. Anything else we should know about Liz?"

"I have not told Arun yet. Only Sally knows. I will be moving into my new apartment in the surgery tomorrow, and Sally will be cooking my dinner as well. She mentioned the strict instructions about his vegetarian cooking, and I agreed to stick to vegetarian as well. Now you all know that I will be moving out tomorrow."

Barbara frowned, "The surgery is so near, why stay there? Please stay here, Liz."

"Mum, I will stay there from tomorrow. I am getting Tuesdays and Thursdays off, and those two days I will stay here, and when you are back from work, we will go shopping or to restaurants as we normally do."

Barbara sighed, "In that case, it is okay with me."

Jeff said, "It is fine with me too, Liz, as long as you are happy. Since getting this job, your face is full of smiles, which we like to see. You seemed to have turned a corner and are full of life and confidence. Being around Arun has transformed you immensely. We are all very pleased about it."

The maid announced that dinner was ready, and they moved to the dining room. During dinner, it was only Chris and Liz talking in low tones and giggling frequently. Once dinner was over, they returned to the lounge.

Stephen said: "Arun, I wanted to ask you something. During your first visit, you told Liz that you wanted to talk to her and assured us it had nothing to do with the affairs of the heart. Tell me, what is that you wanted to talk about."

Arun hesitated, "I think this may not be the best time for that discussion."

Barbara urged, "Why not? We are all here. Please do tell us what is bothering you."

Liz added, "I think I know what you are going to refer to, Arun. Let us deal with it right now."

Arun went on to say, "Two things I became aware of: firstly, that there exists a core group of 10-12 people who are against me because I'm colored, and they want to get rid of me as GP for this area. Secondly, of the 12 or so, four are women, and the leader of the group is reputed to be a wealthy woman, and all in the group do as she bids.

This information has bothered me since I heard it for about two weeks or so after I came to the Village. Of course, I thought it was you, Liz, but not anymore.

A few days ago, I understood Stephen, you are prominent here, and there is nothing you do not know about the village.

I would like to have some clarity on this issue. Even unpleasant answers will not make me change any of the decisions that I have made – and your jobs are safe no matter what you tell me. I appreciate whatever information you can give me."

Stephen sighed, "So these gossips have reached your ears. You do know that several people in the Village like you and are very loyal to you as well. I, too, have heard about this 'hate group' who have strong apartheid-type feelings."

Arun said, "I am surprised that for a person who is supposed to have an ear to the ground, you did not mention or seem to know that the group has been meeting regularly at various premises in the pretext of a charity fundraiser, etc. The police officer who mentioned it is tracking the group to find details of the next meeting and find the principal participants."

Liz said: "Arun, let me own up. I was their leader, and we were meeting at different places, just as you said. After you saved our lives, I decided to leave the group. When I told them that they were sad and disappointed. Some even threatened that I would come to harm, even throw acid in my face. I have not attended any meetings since. They are out of my radar. I am deeply sorry for not telling you this earlier. I suspected then that this would be this matter. What amazes me is that you did not show any bitterness towards me despite your suspicions."

Stephen said shamefacedly: "I am sorry for not coming clean, I was trying to dismantle the group. I knew Liz was their head, and she told me, even before the accident, that she wanted to quit because it was a bad cause, making her uncomfortable. Now there are only three men in the group fostering hatred, but their wives have assured me that their evening visits to the pubs will not happen for the next three months. As the landlords of the pub said about no visits by the group for weeks, and that is the end of that group. Please let us move on from here in a friendly way."

Arun said, "You will always be my friends, and that affection between us will never disappear. The best thing that happened to me is to meet you all, and I'm delighted you are all working for the surgery. There are many things I want to do, but we will discuss them on another day. Trust and have faith in me. I do not change easily."

Liz assured him, "Arun, we have full trust in you, and I have more than that, which I will explain on another day. I'm curious. Knowing that I was the head of the hate group, why did you hire me as your PA?"

"It is usually said, 'keep your friends close, but your enemies closer.' I am a very selfish person, oozing with jealousy. If I find anything useful, I like to keep it to myself, and I will not let it go from my sight."

Chris said, "Liz and Arun, you are both speaking in riddles. Arun, I am glad that there are no contentious issues. Is there anything else to discuss?"

Arun said, "Stephen, I was talking to Dick about gathering all the children and young adults up to 25 years of age one day, as an Open Day. He said there is always a gathering on the Bank Holiday due next Monday. I want both Chris and Liz to extend themselves in organizing this group into two sections: children up to 12 years of age and 13 to 25-year-olds. I want to discuss with both of them, the plans I have."

Barbara said, "You three can go up to the study and talk. Shall I send you some coffee?"

In the study, Arun: continued, "I want you two to prepare a questionnaire about how the children and young adults in those age groups want to make their living in the village. Whatever each one wants is to do regarding further studies, job training, art, music, etc. to be listed on that questionnaire. We will then process them and layout in simple terms the facilities the Village needs to create to make those things happen."

Liz commented, "That is the easy part. What about the cost, time, and effort involved in providing those facilities? Why not give a questionnaire to all the people coming to the village park, so that they can also express what facilities they need?"

Chris added, "What about the time we have to put in to process these questionnaires, and will we be involved in the follow-up? It sounds like a huge project."

Arun said, "I agree with Liz that it has to include all those attending the gathering. We will put your granddad and grandma in charge of that.

We have to do micromanagement – one small step at a time. We have to give the young ones hope so that they stay here and allow the village to grow. You both have key roles in the surgery, but by the time this happens, you both would have moved up and have people under you to delegate to, enabling you two to manage bigger things."

"What about you, Arun?"

"I will still be the Village GP with you two helping me, along with the rest of your family. Nothing too big for me to take care of."

Chris laughed, "Trying to be modest, aren't you, Arun?"

Liz said, "Arun, we will support you to the hilt. I may even do more than that! But please protect yourself with some funds and don't invest everything in these social projects."

Arun replied, "I am anything but modest. If there was a prize for humility and it should go to you and Liz, I would contest it saying I am humbler than either of you! I expect you to exercise your prudence and protect me with regards to my future and protecting myself."

Chris raised an eyebrow, "Am I detecting some intense flirting between you two? Whatever the future holds for both of you, I wish you well. I'm sure the village is a far better place for your arrival here, Arun, I hope we both play a significant part in making your plans a success."

Chris got up and gave Arun a huge hug. Liz did too, went a step further, kissed him on both cheeks, and said those were for the Mini Estate. Chris grinned and said to Arun that if he was planning on visiting anyone else before going to the surgery, he should wipe the lipstick marks from his cheeks. Liz took a tissue and wiped them off a blushing Arun while her parents and grandparents looked on indulgently. After that, Arun said goodnight and left.

Barbara said, "Girls let us talk in this room for some time. Liz, is Arun trying to woo you?

"No, mum. If he wants to woo me, he will say it clearly. He does not know the nuances of subtlety in these things."

Chris raised an eyebrow, "In this short time, you seem to know him quite well; how come?"

"When he spoke to us on the importance of nonverbal communication. I got interested and browsed through his books on the topic."

"And? What did you find, sis?"

"It was there for you all to notice... when you hug Arun, he does not move his hands to hug you back. When you give him a peck, he does not present his cheek as we people here normally do. He is too shy and seems uncomfortable with public displays of affection. When he told me about giving me a new Mini, I reached out spontaneously and squeezed his hand, but he did not reciprocate. That means either he is too shy or there is some sadness in his heart, which we don't know. Or perhaps, it's cultural. As we saw in South Africa, Indians are very cautious. It is a slow process of learning for me."

Barbara said gently, "Arun is an exceptional person to have as a friend, but for anything beyond that, one has to think carefully."

Stephen said, "I agree with your mother, Liz."

"I do not know why you are all panicking and putting me on the defensive. I'm just myself, and if and when such a situation arises, you will all know well in advance. For now, please do not read too much into these gestures."

Chris said thoughtfully, "Mum, I agree with Liz. Maybe this is how we put pressure on her before about her opinions on 'colored' people. Let's all back off. If you start with the warnings, then Liz will not confide in us anymore. At present, she is open about her feelings, and that is how she should be. Don't rush to slap her down."

Jessica said, "I agree with you, Chris. Stephen always has to be first with his opinion without any sensitivity. We should let you two to be free and take life as it comes. Your upbringing will ensure that you make decisions after careful analysis only. Inter-caste, inter-class and international relationships are complex but are now becoming the order of the day. There are excellent people in all communities, and Arun is a gem. I will not put doubt in Liz's mind. Let her be herself."

Liz hugged Jessica, "Thank you, Grandma, for those kind words and the trust you place in both of us. We will not disappoint you. When the time comes, we will choose the best partners for ourselves."

Then Barbara and Jessica were hugged by the girls, and after bidding goodnight, they went to bed. Chris said to Liz when they were alone, that she was too excited to go to sleep and could talk for a while. They had done this several times before, talking till the early hours of the morning. That was when they had no jobs to go to, but tomorrow they had to report to work at the surgery. Liz decreed that they would chat for no more than an hour. They went to Liz's bedroom and climbed into her king-sized bed.

Chris said, "Liz, from what you told me and what I have seen… you do love him, don't you?"

Liz smiled, "It must look that way, but I sincerely feel that he is not keen on flirting or making a move towards me. Something is holding him back. Even when I've made my intentions clear – like swinging the car around to make him fall on my side, he just turned it into a joke."

"Hmm…I am surprised at that. White boys would have taken you or me to bed by now, and he is not even keen on holding your hand. Do you think something is wrong with him?"

Liz frowned, "I don't think so. It may be his Indian upbringing; we know nothing about that. Maybe they do don't make a move until they are married!"

"But he is on his own with nobody watching him. What is the problem then?"

"Still, the effects of upbringing do not change just because one is alone and has the freedom to do anything. Arun sticks to his food habits, for instance. Anyway, I've decided not to push it but study him slowly over the next few weeks."

Chris said," I was upset with mum's warnings – but I'm glad Grandma spoke out for us. She was downright practical. One wonders why mothers behave differently and are too strict but become liberal and reasonable when they become grandmothers."

"She saved the day. Otherwise, I would have blown up and said something that I might have regretted. I like people to say things which I have not done."

"I would like to talk to Arun tomorrow when we three are alone like we did today. Do you mind?"

"Chris, not at all. I would also like to know his mind and where he stands."

On that note, they both went to sleep.

CHAPTER 14

Introspection

The next morning Liz came to the surgery with her luggage to occupy the apartment designated for her use. She arrived early with her mum and Chris, and they found the apartment quite big with lots of cupboards, tables, and comfy furniture. Even though Barbara did not like Liz to stay in the surgery when her house was so nearby, she decided to listen to her mum and give Liz more freedom.

The day was routine for all, and when the time came for the last patient to leave, Chris told Arun that he had to go with her and Liz to the house for dinner to discuss various issues about the meeting in the park. With only a week to go, there were a lot of questions to be sorted out.

"If you were to ask me, you need to come with us every evening until the bank holiday is over," Chris declared. Arun agreed to the suggestion as he wanted to get the job done well.

They reached the house by 6:30 PM, and Barbara and Jeff welcomed them. They all had drinks.

Arun said, "Liz and Chris, here are the questionnaires for the two age groups – Chris you take on the under -12's and Liz, you do the 13-25-years. I have one more for Stephen and Jessica to handle the other people who attend on that day. Are they coming this evening?"

Barbara said, "They will be here by 7:00 PM as Stephen has a meeting with the Village committee (VC) regarding the bank holiday gathering."

Arun said, "Meanwhile, Liz and Chris, why don't you go to the study and spend this time looking through the questionnaires if I've missed out something."

They agreed, and Arun left with Barbara and Jeff.

Barbara said, "Arun, you are trying to achieve a lot by yourself. Please leave it to the VC to manage whatever it is you want to do."

Arun said nicely, "Barbara, the Village Committee has been here all along, and these questionnaires will hardly make a difference to their conception of the project, it's execution and financing. I can understand involving the VC in this, but not transferring the responsibility to them. I hope you will support me on this."

Jeff said, "You are right, Arun. If you leave it to them, they will make a mess of it. They have a lot of experience in that area!"

Meanwhile, Stephen and Jessica came in and went through the questionnaires with Chris and Liz.

Stephen said, "Arun, we have seen the survey, and the questions are fine. Most of the work has to be done on the day persuading people to participate actively and even helping them fill out the forms. Both Liz and Chris will have their work cut out."

Arun said, "I will be presenting my ideas for consideration by the Village people and to the committee. I have been thinking about the issues for weeks. The projects will involve the usual 3M's – money, materials, and management. Of course, it has to be a joint effort, with the Village Committee playing a crucial role. For the moment, today's' task is done, and thank you all for that."

The maid announced that dinner was ready, and they departed to the dining room. After dinner, they assembled again in the lounge.

Chris spoke up, "Arun, I'd like to ask a personal question and hope you do not mind. Does your cultural background still affect how you behave in our so-called liberated society?"

Arun said thoughtfully, "There is no short answer for this. In India, where I was born and brought up, society had strict norms about how boys and girls behaved with their parents, elders, and amongst themselves. A lot of behavior considered natural here is taboo. One should not be speaking to a girl in school or college, and any interaction between sexes is discouraged.

Youngsters have to be very obedient and respectful in their speech and actions when it comes to parents and elders, related to them or not. No insubordination tolerated. Liberated attitudes towards touching, dating, going to cafes, hugging, and kissing are not allowed. Even in cinemas, the film Censors remove kissing scenes.

Clothes too, especially for ladies, have to be modest – no low-cut blouses, mini-skirts and the like. Boys and girls will not have any experience of touching, kissing, or sex until they are married. I am talking about the majority of the families.

Of course, the oldest profession in the world is widely prevalent in India as well. In fact, in olden days, many temples had court dancers who used to be of service exclusively to the landlords, priests, and members of influence in society. Despite these practices, when it comes to an average boy or girl – anyone from a respectable family, should not be seen hanging around with the other gender in public.

So, Chris, it does affect my behavior, and I have not changed one bit in the last few years of being in London."

Liz asked, "So, if a lady were to touch your hand and give you a peck on the cheek, will you reciprocate or shy away?"

Arun smilingly said, "I was surprised when those situations happened to me in the last few days. Honestly, I was embarrassed. Then I told myself that one: in this country, it is the usual response to show appreciation for any act and two: there is always the crucial issue of being colored. One has to be extremely careful not to cross the boundaries of good behavior. For instance, even if the person involved may not mind a similar response, the other people who are watching might detest this, and it might reflect unfavorably on both persons involved.

Hence, I failed to respond on such occasions, and I am sorry if that was hurtful."

Barbara asked, "How would you react if a girl in this country has a crush on you and would like to take things further?"

"I have to be very careful how I phrase this reply," Arun said blushing. "There are times I hate myself for being what I am, but I cannot change quickly. I will expect the girl I see as my future life partner to conform to certain things. Not to hug and cuddle with other men, be they, friends or strangers, not to dance with them or get physical. For my part, I will only dance with my wife, and I would prefer her to dance only with me. I have avoided going to any dances despite invitations for this reason. I usually leave before the dancing begins, giving some excuse. As a medic, I have gotten away with it so far.

In these aspects, I am not a social animal and any sensible girl knowing this should avoid me like the plague. I am not proud of this attitude, but I have decided to live with it for better or worse!"

There was silence for a while, then Liz asked, "Hypothetically, following my mum's question earlier, if I were to show such an interest in you, how would you react?"

Arun responded, "It is not that easy to give a 'yes' or 'no' answer. Sometimes what the heart feels, one may not be able to reveal quickly. But I will try to reply.

For this, I need to tell you about the Hindu religion. Unlike Christianity and Islam, which have only one God – Jesus, the son of God, or Allah, respectively, the Hindu religion is more like a corporate conglomerate. There are three main gods – triumvirates, with their wives, the principal goddesses.

We have, therefore, many Gods and several Sub-Gods and demi-Gods. Like in the corporate world, one cannot offend anybody; one must understand and satisfy the 'powers that be' to make any mark in the organization.

Then, there is the principle of Karma, which, to simplify, means that what you do in this life follows you into the next life. What you are in this world is due to what you did in your last lifecycle. I will explain what this has to do with us.

The first time I saw you, Liz, you were so beautiful, and I could also perceive that you were from a wealthy family. I thought that this is due to your good Karma accrued in your previous birth, you have benefitted in this birth from the blessing of the three principal Goddesses.

From Goddess Lakshmi, you have inherited beauty; from her assistant Kubera you have affluent parents. From Goddess Saraswathi, you have inherited a good education. From Goddess Parvati, who has the gift of courage and a fighting spirit – which frankly alarmed me. I wanted you to be near me, but then, I did not know how to calm you, as I knew nothing about you. The accident allowed me to prove that I was not such a bad guy after all.

Coming back to your question, you are in a position which millions of girls dream of – beautiful and precious. As we say in India, Mount Meru, you are at the top of a fictional mountain, which is the tallest of all mountains. You should be looking up and aiming for the stars. Find a match, a son of a prominent industrialist, MP, or even a Lord with secure connections. Why should you look downwards instead and choose a person like me?

Then there is the issue of my color. That has its complications. We both may overlook it, but what about our offspring? The world they would grow up may not be kind or understanding. They would be subject to ridicule and hearing words to hurt them. After all, children are the cruelest in many ways.

Finally, what about your parents' dreams for you? If they do not agree with this match, you might lose them, your family connections, your friends, and your inheritance. Is it worth it?

Can we just stay professional friends is a question that plagues my mind? But being possessive, that's not enough for me. I find that on an issue so fundamental, I am very selfish.

I am not sure whether I have done justice to your query Liz. At this point, I cannot say the right course of action. I can only speak my heart. Regardless of how I feel, be assured that I will never cross the line and embarrass you and your parents and grandparents. One needs all their blessings.

I hope I have not assumed too much from your comments about taking it to the limit. Otherwise, it would make an 'ass of u and me' as they say in the USA of the word assume. For me, 'the limit' means a life partner, and on that basis, I have replied. If you did not say that, then I am sorry for being presumptuous."

Liz said gently, "I did mean that as the 'limit,' and thank you for the very candid explanations. You have spoken quite clearly on the issues involved and your emotions as an Indian faced with such cultural differences."

Chris said, "Arun, you are so quiet but equally, a very complex character. I am sure you will find a way when 'the limit' does become a reality."

Barbara broke the spell, "Why talk of hypothetical situations now? Let us talk of other things regarding the bank holiday and the menus for the day and what we have to do to succeed."

Jessica broke in, "Here you go again, Barbara, burying your head in the sand and dreaming that all will be as you planned for your daughters."

Arun said, "I will let you get on with the menus and the planning. I will return to the surgery. A lot of introspection, mostly unsolicited, because I could have shortened my replies. However, I wanted you all to know the real me. If I happen to be a disappointment to you all, I do not blame you – I know my shortcomings very well. That's why I prefer to focus more on my work and charity. Thank you for all your patience."

Stephen clapped him on the back and said: "You are one in a million. We appreciate your frankness, especially your concerns about bridging the two cultures with racial overtones exacerbated by the people around them. It was very touching and illuminating to me and, I am sure, to all the others."

Arun shook his hand, "Thank you, Stephen. And thank you, Barbara, for dinner. I will see you all in the morning at the Surgery."

With that, he was about to leave.

Liz said, "How charming! Arun, you have forgotten that I am going to stay in the Surgery from today, and I am supposed to drive you back!"

Arun apologized when all others laughed at his omission. They said their goodbyes and left.

When they entered the Surgery, they went upstairs and were facing the respective doors to their apartments when suddenly Liz turned and said: "Enough of riddles. Let me do what I've wanted to do." She planted a massive kiss on his mouth and pressed his head towards hers forcibly. Arun was stunned but, being a man, he had to reciprocate, and this cuddling and kissing went on for a few minutes until they both were breathless.

"What is the point of worrying about differences in culture? To hell with cultures and their restrictions," Liz said breathlessly. "Let us satisfy our basic instincts. I am going to be very wicked with you from now on. You don't object, do you, Arun?"

"Now that you and I have crossed the limit let us not retrace our steps. Let us continue beyond the 'limit' wickedly."

He pulled her into his arms and planted his lips on hers. Liz, too reciprocated. With difficulty, they pulled apart after a while, and Arun suggested that it was time to go to their apartments, and she smilingly agreed. She had stars in her eyes, and he saw problems ahead for both of them.

CHAPTER 15

Focusing on Priorities

It was a busy day for Arun and Chris at the Surgery. Arun had asked a senior nurse to come to the Surgery and show Chris and Jessica the ropes. Chris underwent training for the first two hours, followed by Jessica. Chris needed to attend a few additional courses on nursing and travel vaccinations. Chris also needed further training on dealing with diabetic and asthmatic patients and on specialized procedures for ante- and postnatal clinics. Chris found that the scope of her role had become vast.

There was a mail-in her in-tray from Arun about an increase in pay for the additional workload. She was delighted to receive the note on her salary rise, which put her earnings on par with big city surgeries. Chris wanted to share her joy with the family, but she knew that Arun did not like family meetings during the Surgery, except during the lunch hour when all staff would be present, including Dave and Sally. She curtailed her enthusiasm and consoled herself that she would tell them in the evening. She would have to thank Arun sometime in the morning in the Surgery.

Barbara had a lot of letters to type, and she was out of everyone's way the whole day. Liz was busy with the leaflets she brought from the hospital and was reading up about the clinic Arun ran at the hospital. She thought for a while about the special moments she had shared last night with Arun – but there's more to come tonight, she grinned.

At the lunch break, Arun rushed through his lunch and left to see Mr. Ted Baker, the estate agent.

Ted said, "Doctor, I have just the property you wanted. It is next door to the Surgery. Mrs. Heather Dawson owns the bungalow. Her husband died two years ago, and her daughter in Yorkshire has asked her to live with them. She wants to make a quick sale. The house was put on the market last week for GBP 15000. Are you keen on this property? Do you want me to negotiate? I can get her to knock off a few thousand from the asking price."

"Mr. Baker, I am grateful to you for letting me know about the bungalow. If I like it, I will pay the asking price. No need to distress the old lady in her hour of sorrow. When can we go and see the place?"

"Doctor, we can go now if you can spare 15 -20 minutes."

Arun agreed, and they went to see the bungalow. A few people saw them entering the place, including Barbara and Liz. Arun knew that they would want details. He inspected the house and liked it. He noticed some damp patches but thought that Dave could fix it quickly.

Arun told Ted, "Mr. Baker, I agree to the price. I want to sign the contract ASAP."

"The contract can be signed, and the deeds transferred within a month," Ted assured him.

"I am very pleased. Is it possible to have the keys to enter the bungalow for a day so that Dave can see what repairs are needed?"

Ted agreed to this. Arun thanked him and left for the Surgery. Barbara and Liz gave him questioning looks, but he pretended not to notice and went to his consulting room. At the closing hour, Chris walked into his office.

"Thank you, Doctor, for the generous raises, totally unexpected and most welcome. I am indebted to you for that and for investing in my training."

"It is part of the job requisites for anybody who wants to make senior nurse in a year. You have the right qualifications, commitment, and motivation – the rest will follow as you go."

"You are so good to me and us all. Thank you. You are coming home tonight for dinner for the next few days till the bank holiday, aren't you?"

"Sure. Let Sally have a few days break from cooking my dinner."

Barbara joined them, "We saw you going into the bungalow. Are you buying it? What are the plans?"

"Let' talk about it when we are all at your home this evening," said Arun.

That evening when they all met in Barbara's house, Barbara told Jessica, Stephen, and Jeff about Arun going to the bungalow next door to the Surgery.

"We are all itching to know the details from the man of the moment."

Arun said, "I asked Ted, the estate agent, to give me first refusal whenever a property came on the market. He left a message yesterday that the elderly owner was selling as she had decided to live with her daughter in Yorkshire. The agent showed me the bungalow, which I liked instantly, and I agreed to pay the full amount quickly so that she can leave the village in a happy frame of mind. ."

Chris said, "If I am not so inquisitive, why the bungalow and what for?"

"You are very pleasantly curious, and that is what we have gathered here to discuss. I have permission from the NHS top brass to set up a consultancy for ophthalmology here. So, besides the hospital, I can see my patients here, and Liz will oversee them. The accounts for the private practice will be entirely separate from those of the NHS surgery."

Liz: asked, "Am I going to be a nomad for a few months until the bungalow is ready?"

"I asked Ted to give the keys to Dave for a day next week to discuss modifications. I would like you, Liz, to get involved as it means rooms for you as well. Dave should be able to make the changes quickly, starting with your office room so that you can relocate there, when the other renovations will be going on, and you will have to put up with the inconvenience."

Barbara: "Why move now, Liz? Why not wait for a few weeks?"

"I agree with mum. Why should I move out so soon?"

Arun raised a hand, "Please trust me. It is good for both of us. Even though Stephen said that the 'racist' group now consists of just three men, I had to act swiftly – especially now, as our relationship is also developing a lot faster than my Surgery plans! I'd like to know whether you gave up your leadership post in writing or verbally. If verbally, I request you to put it in writing for posterity."

Liz: frowned, "I had done it verbally, as we always did about meeting places and the agendas for the meetings. I did not think of any complications arising from it. I have had no contact with them, but I will draft a letter to the group, as you wish.

Arun said, "Please do and then issue it to the existing members with individual copies to the members who have left. Make sure you state your intentions clearly."

Chris said, "Getting back to the bungalow. Will it also contain an apartment for Liz?"

"Yes, there will be an extension on the side with two similar apartments, one on each floor, for her and me."

"Arun, that's a charming plan. What about the two apartments now occupied by you two?"

"Necessity is the mother of all inventions. With me also moving there, no one can accuse us of misconduct on the surgery premises. This bungalow is my property, not owned by NHS and, hence, Liz, and I do not have to answer to anybody."

Arun continued, "Chris, regarding the two apartments in the Surgery, you can have one when we move out. The other is for your suitor; someone working in the village who will not take you away and deprive us of your experience and company."

"So, you are looking for a suitor for me then?"

Arun smiled, "Let the Bank Holiday event pass, and then we can discuss it."

Chris laughed, "I do not want to be kept in suspense. Whom have you earmarked for me?"

Arun: "As it happens, I do have someone in mind. Bob Smith used to work for me in London as a Manager for a short time. He is handsome and quite brilliant at his job. He's very keen on moving here and working with me – so, no doubt, you will meet him shortly."

Chris sighed dramatically, "After that description! I am bound to have sleepless nights from now on till I meet him in person. Is he due here on the bank holiday?"

Arun: "I am not sure, but when I know, I will tell you."

"If he is as good as you say, then it is up to Chris to rope him. Anyway, let us wait for things to develop. Once again, Arun to the rescue!" Barbara smiled.

Liz asked, "Whom have you chosen for me?"

Arun smilingly said: "You are an independent person with an independent mind. I am sure you will sort yourself out soon."

The maid announced that dinner was ready, and they went to the dining room. After dinner, they returned to the lounge for coffee.

Jessica said, "Arun, we are indebted to you! The generosity of your heart is stupendous. May the Lord bless you with everything and remove all obstacles in your way."

"Thank you for your blessings and words of kindness. I do have one more thing to say, and it involves Liz. The new Mini Estate is due for delivery at 10:00 AM tomorrow. You can collect it and drive your mum to work if you wish."

Chris asked, "Will I ever get a car from the surgery?"

"Sorry, Chris, NHS funding does not allow it! But I tell you what, once you have demonstrated your skills with the patients, in a year I can make you a minor partner with 1/3 of the profits of the Surgery after expenses. Once you are a partner, you can have your car with its expenses covered by NHS funding. It is unusual to have a nurse as a partner, but the decision rests with the senior partner."

Chris, whooped, "I am so happy, Arun, and I will put in maximum effort to satisfy the patients and, more importantly, my senior partner!"

Meanwhile, Liz spent her time browsing through the mini estate's papers – the invoice, insurance, road tax, etc. She was stunned to notice the license plate number: 65LIZ01 (year 65 and the first car of Liz). She was so thrilled. She forgot where she was and planted a kiss on his mouth. Arun released her quickly and told her to calm down. It was only a car that belonged to the business, and she can use it as long as she works for Surgery.

Liz beamed, "Sorry everybody for that spontaneous display of emotion on seeing the number plate – very thoughtfully chosen. Chris, please see the brochure and then pass it on."

Liz: continued, "Sorry, Arun, to embarrass you. Our culture is all about the spontaneous expression of happiness compared to your culture with its too reserved attitude and very delayed responses. Let us leave for the Surgery. I am sorry everybody for an upsetting protocol. Goodnight."

As they left, the family was speechless and looked at Barbara, who wondered whether she ought to have brought up her daughters with a greater sense of dignity.

Jessica said briskly, "Well, Barbara, it has happened, and we all have to take things as they come. I remember the song *Que Sara Sara, whatever will be, will be; the future is not ours to see, Que Sara Sara.*"

They all laughed, except Barbara, who had a very concerned look. "Does anybody know how to stop a runaway train, like Liz?"

Chris said, "Calm down, mum; Liz is grown up, and if you want her happiness, then let her go where her heart lies."

Barbara was far from convinced but knew she was the odd one out – so she held her peace. And shortly afterward, everyone dispersed for the night.

In the car, Liz did not say much, but her face revealed her excitement. When they got to their apartments, she burst out: "I need to talk to you, Mister! What do you mean by pushing me next door when the renovation work is taking place?"

Arun: "The quicker we move out of this property for which NHS pay monthly rent, etc., the better for us. Otherwise. they would think I am misusing those privileges. Where would you sleep unless you go back to your place?"

"What about in your apartment?"

Arun sighed, "Liz, be sensible. We want to take all the precautions so that no one suspects too much."

She pulled him forcibly to her and kissed him. "I want to be with you, and I couldn't care less about the others."

"Patience is a virtue; please wait for a couple of months. We can move out. Meanwhile, nothing stops us from discussing work in my apartment until you go to the bungalow."

"There's only one type of business I like discussing after 10:00 PM," Liz said mischievously.

Arun grinned, "You'd better send the letter for the hate group tomorrow, if possible."

Liz nodded in agreement. Arun said, 'good girl' and gave her a big hug and a kiss. After several minutes they parted and went to their apartment.

CHAPTER 16

Sleepwalking

Liz could not sleep. So many things had happened to make her happy and to dream about it. However, Arun's concerns about the group and its current three members also worried her. She was tossing and turning in bed. At 11:30 PM, she felt she had to speak to Arun. Wearing only a thin nightgown, she went up to his apartment and twisted the knob. The door opened. She tiptoed to Arun's bed. He opened his eyes and saw her beautiful body outlined in the nightgown.

Arun blinked. "What are you doing? Sleepwalking? What time is it?"

Liz purred, "Darling, I could not sleep. I am too excited about the car and us staying in the new bungalow. And I'm too worried about the three bad men! I can't sleep, and I need someone to cuddle up to."

"You came wearing this. Don't you think it might lead to actions we might regret later?"

"On the contrary, I will treasure it and want more."

She slipped out of her nightgown, snuck under the covers, and started caressing him. Arun had not expected this.

"Liz!" he whispered urgently, trying to capture her straying hands, "We have to be mature about these things, don't you think?"

"I'm ready to do mature things! That is why I am naked – for you to act."

"Liz, please stop being silly."

"No! Stop talking and let us behave more maturely." She started unbuttoning his pajamas.

Despite Arun's s objections, he was soon hopelessly lost, and they drifted into a different world of ecstasy. He never thought he would bed her so soon while she wondered why it had taken them so long. They were locked in rapture till they fell asleep cuddling and slept till 7:00 AM. Arun was shocked as he rarely slept beyond 5:00 AM. In 30 minutes, Sally would be there. He woke Liz up, made her put on her nightgown, and run to her bedroom. Arun got ready in about 25 minutes and went down to see Sally enter the surgery. He wished her good morning and went to his office. Sally said she would bring him coffee in a few minutes.

Liz came downstairs around 8:00 AM glowing with happiness. Sally noticed it, and when Liz told about the new car, she thought that this was the reason behind her radiance. Liz went up to Arun's room and was about to knock but changed her mind. The fact that Sally was watching her had a lot to do with her change of mind. She was thinking of last night and how much she enjoyed every second of it. Arun's shyness, Liz, found endearing. She thought of his talk of doing the right thing while doing precisely the opposite and enjoying every bit of it. She adored him and his hypocrisy. She knew he loved her, and he would never try to hurt her ever. He was for life, as far as she was concerned. As he had said some days ago, his life partner was for life, and she knew she was the one. She felt she should act in a similar way towards him. She would never let him down, ever. He had come into her life like a knight in shining armor.

Sally came to ask her if she wanted coffee. Liz realized that in her excitement, she had forgotten about breakfast. She rushed to the dining room to find Arun also in the same situation. They smiled and quickly had cereal and coffee and left for work. Liz had very little to do on that day, besides collecting the appointment lists from the hospital, so she was eagerly anticipating her new car.

The Mini Estate car with the special plate bearing the registration '65 LIZ 01" came in an exclusive carrier, and the vehicle brought it to the ground. There was a huge bouquet, a box of chocolates and a bottle of champagne that came with it. The representative, who was overseeing the delivery, checked the car for any marks or scratches, and he checked the parts by opening the bonnet and boot. After convincing himself that all were in order, he finally got Liz to sign for the car's delivery.

Her mum and Chris came out, and they all went for a short drive. Everything seemed okay to her. She let Chris drive it for a spell, and she liked it as well. For a small car, it handled very well and had a good pick up. They returned in about 45 minutes, and Chris returned to her nursing duties relieving Jessica to go for a ride with Stephen. They also enjoyed the trip. At the lunch break, Liz spoke volumes about the 'small big car' and its handling abilities.

Dave picked up the keys of the bungalow and, accompanied by Liz, went to check the state of repairs needed. The bungalow was in a good nick; the entrance hall and the lobby needed a minimal repair. The living room was large, and that needed to become the main consulting room for Arun. The main bedroom would be an office for Liz. The other two places on the other side of the lobby could be another consulting room and a store. There was a need for an accessible toilet, and the main bathroom had to be modified. The WC would be adequate for general use.

Dave estimated that Liz's office would be ready in a week. The bedroom extensions would take eight weeks after getting the planning permission. He calculated that Liz could move into the bedrooms on the ground floor in two weeks and live there. Arun insisted on total security on all external doors and windows. Liz was happy that Arun was attending to these details without her prompting. Also, Arun said the extension should be a four- bedroomed house with two en-suite bathrooms. He asked Dave to get a drawing prepared for application to the local council ASAP. Arun was happy that things were going well, but Liz had another thought that would scupper all that she thought would tell him later.

Arun and Liz returned to the Surgery to start the afternoon clinic.

Chris was eager to know what happened. The whole family with Arun met in their home at 6:00 PM. With soft drinks in their hands, they looked to him for an update.

Liz set the ball rolling, "The modifications needed are minimal as the bungalow was in good condition. Dave says we can convert the main bedroom into an office, which means only moving furniture; no other change needed. Some of the other rooms need a bit of work. He said I could move into the premises within two weeks of Arun completing the sale."

Arun said, "And that will be much sooner than you think. The old lady is moving all her stuff to Yorkshire tomorrow. Dave will move the bed and other furniture so that you can move into the bungalow as of Monday or Tuesday. However, if you want to choose a better bed and furniture, you can do it next week. You call the shots regarding your move."

"You move very fast, Arun – Speedy Gonzales! Yes, I would like to change the furniture to suit my taste – more feminine looking. So, I will shop tomorrow after dropping you off at the hospital. Chris and mum, please come too, as I would appreciate your advice.

"I would love to come, and mum is nodding as well. What time shall we leave?"

Liz began working it out "Arun's clinics start at 8.30 AM, and he would like to have 30 minutes of preparatory time. Why don't you two go to the shops and do a pre-selection for me to finalize? I will give you a list of things I need. I can meet you both later after I finish at the hospital."

Arun said, "Liz, there will be times when you may not be able to take me to the hospital. So, treat tomorrow as one of those days and go with them once you drop me off. Please take this GBP 2000 and use it for quality furniture. If you need more, use these cheques, which I have signed already. Because these are my cheques, I am paying for it and not the Surgery. All receipts are to be collected and filed for the yearly accounting."

Chris gasped, "You do not mess around, do you? GBP 2000 is a big amount – and signed cheques to cover the extras. I wish someone treated me like that!"

Barbara said, "Liz, let me keep the cheques. Then you two girls can shop without fear of losing or misplacing your handbags. Arun, you are so generous treating Liz like a queen!"

Arun smiled, "She is worth it; don't you all agree? Anyway, regarding the modifications, the extension on the side of the bungalow will be a four-bedroomed apartment on two floors. The entirely new construction, which will take 5-6 months to be complete. I will move to the bungalow once this extension is ready for occupation."

Liz wailed, "I did not realize that you will take so long to move in."

Chris teased, "Sis, you already yearn for him and miss him. Why don't you also move only when the apartment next door is ready?"

"Hmm... maybe that is what I will do. I'll think about it."

The maid announced that the dinner was ready, and after dinner, they returned to the lounge.

Arun said, "Liz, you wanted to give the group members your letter about leaving the group, were you able to manage it?"

"After leaving the bungalow, I collected the letters and gave them to them personally. To the lady members, I explained the reason for the letter. They wanted to copy it and send it to others with their signature so that they could have a written copy of leaving the group. I did not explain to the male members, but I could sense that they guessed what it would be as I had told them already, verbally. The three who are very sensitive about this issue did not comment. Grandpa will give you his views later on in this matter. Whew! I must say I felt very relieved after handing over those letters."

Stephen sighed, "I feel the three are still trouble – more so as others have deserted them. They are angrier with Liz as she was the leader and had financial clout. If they can do damage to her and your reputation, they will. It is not a question of *if*, more an issue of **when** they will do it. Arun, you need to increase the security to the Surgery and the bungalow. The Neighborhood Watch Committee with me as its Chief will also increase our vigilance, but we do not have a legal presence and, therefore, can only take limited action.

Arun asked, "Couldn't you name the three people to the police in confidence so that they can keep track of their movements and prevent them from inflicting damage?"

Liz said, "The typical damages they inflict are damaging car tires, throwing stones through the windows, scratching the cars, sending anonymous threatening letters, and so forth."

Arun: said, "There must be a different way to reach out to these people. If only I could meet them and talk to them on neutral ground. I wonder if you can tell me, Stephen, if any of their folk have any health or eye problems. Tackling those might defuse some of their anger."

"I can try to find out. I'm sure the patients' medical records must be in the village practice."

Arun said, "I have the medical records of the past patients. I need only their names."

Stephen nodded. "I will give them to you on Monday. I need a weekend to scout around for details."

"Thank you, Stephen. I hope we get lucky."

Barbara sighed, "It is getting more and more complicated. It's like being in South Africa during apartheid – this time, it's the whites who are plotting!"

Arun said, "It is not as bad as all that. An unnecessary irritant, but we will deal with it. Anyway, it is time to go home as we need to have an early start."

Then Liz and Arun left for the Surgery.

Arun changed and went to bed with a book to read. But the door opened, and Liz came in a see-through robe like the previous night and slid under the sheets. She quickly undressed them both and pulled him close to her.

Arun whispered, "If you do this every night, I won't be able to sleep without you warming me up. I can't bear the thought of you moving to the bungalow, leaving me alone here. It's not on. I have to do something soon."

"Lover, what are you going to do? Come to the bungalow and sleep with me openly and let everyone know we are misbehaving?"

"Liz, darling, I will think of something more elegant than that."

"What? Marry me now?"

Arun looked at her, "Why not? We are doing what married couples do. I enjoy being educated by you and want to learn more."

"Arun, I want to give you more than what I gave you yesterday, which was more of an adolescent experience – seeing, touching, and kissing. I want to raise the bar on our sexual activity; we should be more adult than an adolescent."

"But Liz, we have other things to consider as well. What about the group and what they will do to us if they know we are together?"

"Arun, why don't you focus on what is in front of you and perform well. Other things can wait. Let us enjoy the present. I am waiting for your actions!"

"You naughty and wicked girl! Who taught you to think and talk like this? I like you and adore you for that. Let me focus, as you say, on what is in front of me."

Liz kissed him and whispered, "Will you stop talking and start behaving like a lover whose love is waiting?"

For the next hour or so, they were in a land of bliss, totally oblivious to cultural taboos and restrictions. They were beyond caring about anyone or anything. The pleasure they experienced was so exquisite that they decided that they had to have it every night; other people's opinions be damned. It was just the two of them, deeply in love. It was due to Liz's bold and brazen actions that the relationship had blossomed so quickly, and all their pentup passion surfaced. Arun loved her and could not think of life without her. Liz felt Arun was the man she was looking for, and his color did not bother her anymore. He was a perfect man, and she wanted to be loyal and faithful to him as he would be to her. He would be a good father to their children, and working for him and with him was the greatest blessing God could have given her.

She decided to buy him a special gift while shopping before buying other things like beds and furniture. The pleasure inside her escalated, and when the final release came, she hugged and kissed him and went into a deep slumber.

CHAPTER 17

Shopping Bonanza

"Arun, what time is it?"

"6:15 AM."

"If we have to leave by 7:30, I have to get up now."

She got out of bed with nothing on. She searched under the sheets for the negligee without luck. She found the shirt of Arun's pajamas, donned it, and left the room in a hurry. She entered her bedroom only to see Chris already waiting there, casting a surprising look at seeing Liz in a man's shirt, emerging from Arun's bedroom!

"Since when have you stopped sleeping here, sis? And where is your nightgown?"

"I have to rush to get ready. My nightgown is under the sheet on Arun's bed! Where else, do you think? Why did you come so early?"

"You answer my question first!"

Liz replied, "Well if you must know, inquisitive sis, since the last two nights. I'm not discussing it any further."

Chris laughed. "Well, I came early in my car. Mum has gone to pick up Gran, who also wants to tag along. I came up to surprise you, and it's I who got the surprise. Did you reward him for the new car with the ultimate prize a girl can give a boy?"

Liz frowned and said, "I have no regrets on that; he enjoyed the reward too. We are going to share his bed from now on. Do not tell anyone."

Chris sat straighter. "You're not serious about this relationship, are you? Is it going to be long-term or just a passionate fling?"

Liz turned to her, "We are going to be married, and I cannot get a better partner than him. He also feels the same. I am looking out for two special items on our shopping trip, and you and I will have to sneak away from the rest and buy them."

Chris sat up agog. "Sure, I can manage that. What items are they – not rings, surely?"

"Yes, rings, they are! Even Arun does not know yet. I am going to surprise him tonight."

Chris asked archly, "Should I anticipate another riotous night for you both? Enjoy, but take precautions for now."

"Don't forget he is a GP and has preventives at hand, like those you carry in your handbag."

Chris yelped, "Sis, it is naughty of you to snoop around in my handbag. I had not used them for a long time – maybe four years ago when I went to South Africa. A one-night stand. I regret it now, but I enjoyed it at that time. No more of those for me. From now on, I'm going to hold out until I find a life partner like you."

Liz said, "I hope the person Arun mentioned for you is a good one and, if you like him, go for him. Arun is a good judge of character."

Chris looked at her, speculatively, "I am amazed at the sudden transformation you have had in such a short time. When you met Arun in the shop, you were such a racist. I am very proud of you, sis."

"It is true. I have changed because Arun trusted in me and his refusal to believe the worst. He has helped us find our way and help the Village, which we have never done before."

Chris said, "I am so much impressed with you that I would dearly love to emulate you. I'll take your advice about Arun's recommendations, but whether it works with him or someone else, I would like to firm up on my life partner soon, as you have, and spend quality married life working for the good of the community. Arun has got all of us thinking about what's best for the community in a way we have never done before.

We might have funded projects but have not cared for the community as Arun does, and I am sure he will achieve much with or without our help. Anyway, time to leave – come on."

They met the others, and after a quick coffee, they left, intending to have breakfast in the hospital canteen.

When Arun was alone in the car with Liz, he asked: "Aren't you going to tell me what you talked about with Chris that kept us all waiting?"

Liz grinned. "She got very nosy when she caught me wearing your shirt this morning. I told her that I had decided that you were my life partner, and that meant we would be sleeping together for the rest of our lives."

Arun said, "I admire your candid comments, and I must say, Liz, I am blessed to have you as my life partner as well. I promise you that I will smother you with so much love and affection that it may suffocate you. If I could, I would marry you today itself in the hospital's church so that we no longer have to hide it from others."

Liz: raised an eyebrow, "Do they perform weddings in the hospital church?"

"Well, I just said that to make a point about marrying you ASAP. Of course, in the hospital, one has to be seriously ill for a wedding. You may lose out a lot if your mum and dad cut you off from your inheritance because of our marriage."

"Oh, I doubt if they will go so far. Mum and dad might not like it, but they will have to get used to it. If choosing you as my life partner means giving up my inheritance, then that inheritance is not worth it. The biggest treasure for me is YOU, and that will not change until I die."

Arun said tenderly, "You are so sweet, Liz. Financially, we will have a lot more than we can spend. Of course, our mission is to work for the community, which means we should not show off wealth as celebrities do.

I did take a salary cut coming here. But what I lost in revenue is nothing compared to finding the real treasure here, the Kohinoor Diamond – YOU! We will have enough money to live happily and let us enjoy doing public service and raise our children with ethical values and morals. Whatever I earn is for us both to use. You will have access to all my accounts – my account, joint account, and business account. However, you can keep your finances separate."

"Thank you, Arun, for making such generous suggestions. I will also operate my account as a joint account only. I do not believe in the principle of, 'whatever's yours is mine, and whatever's mine is also mine!'"

Arun changed the topic, "Liz, I hesitated to ask you before and hope you do not mind. But why is it that your mum is stricter in the way she talks to you compared to how she speaks to Chris? And why is it that your dad does not want to come to the Surgery? I am also not sure about your grandpa – about his motives – whereas Jessica is straight and to the point. With her, what you see is what you get."

Liz said as she pulled up, "Here we are? I'll answer your questions on the return journey if we are traveling alone."

They got out of the car and went into the hospital. Arun went to his room, and Liz went to the canteen to meet the others.

"Mum, let's watch Arun perform the first operation and then go to the canteen. I hope it won't put you off your food. It's a complex surgery, and you can judge the intricate work he has specialized in all these years in London."

They all agreed and went to the room where there was a monitor used for training the students and junior doctors. Few people came in on the weekend, so they had the place to themselves. The operation they watched was quite intricate, and they marveled at how Arun could carry out such work multiple times a day. His hands must be so steady and eyesight quite clear. They could not believe how quickly 30 minutes went by.

After breakfast, they went shopping. The biggest shop in the area stocked a large amount of furniture and homeware. They spent an hour there, choosing a bed, sheets, covers, and pillows. They were quite expensive, but the top of the range and Arun had told her to buy the best (for them, which Liz omitted to mention)! They went to another store specializing in modern bedroom furniture and bought a wardrobe, chest of drawers, dressing table with an attractive mirror, a couple of stools, and other odds and ends. By then, it was time for lunch.

Liz said, "Usually, I have lunch with Arun. Do you all want to have lunch in a nice café? I will join you in an hour."

Chris said, "You do not like to leave Arun alone even for a moment, do you? I think it is better you go to the hospital. As his PA, he may have some queries, and you must take care of those."

Barbara was quite happy to go to a café rather than eat at the hospital canteen. They agreed to meet in a popular restaurant, which Liz and Chris frequented. Liz returned to the hospital to meet Arun in the cafeteria.

While returning to meet Arun, she mused on how she had gotten into the habit of having every meal with Arun. How strange, she thought, that in such a short time she had changed so much. Fancy places did not seem to matter so much to her now than to be with him all the time.

Arun said, after she had told him about the morning's shopping, "Liz, ever since we got to know each other well, I always want to be with you and have breakfast, lunch, and dinner with you and not on my own. I am glad you returned, and I am hoping you feel the same."

She squeezed his hand in response. After lunch, they sneaked into his office for a passionate kiss before she left to join the others.

She met her family in the café in time for a cup of coffee.

Chris observed, "Hmm… sis, your lipstick is smudged all over!"

Liz frowned at her and excused herself to go to the bathroom. She remembered Arun telling her not to put on any makeup as she was beautiful without it. With a vengeance, she removed all the lipstick from her lips, washed her face thoroughly, dried her face, and then returned to the table.

Chris frowned "Why, Liz, you have removed all your makeup!"

"I had decided from now on not to use any as per doctor's orders. Cosmetics ruin the skin!"

Barbara remarked, "It is nice to know that you won't be wasting 20 -30 minutes every morning and evening doing up your face."

They all laughed and sipped their coffee. Liz paid the bill.

"Mum, why don't Chris and I do some browsing while you and Grandma relax here? We'll meet here again in an hour if it is okay with you all?"

Barbara raised an enquiring eyebrow but decided not to pursue it. "Well, we may do some shopping of our own. Alright, see you later."

Liz took Chris to the most expensive jewelry shop, making sure that the elders were out of sight before it.

Chris nudged her. "What exactly are you looking for?"

"Wedding rings for Arun and me."

"What? You are moving fast, aren't you? Do you have his finger size?"

"Arun removes his ring on the days he has operations to perform. I took it from the drawer without his knowledge. He doesn't know I'm going to buy the rings today, but I know he will agree to whatever I say."

Chris sighed, "I am growing more and more envious of you, sis. Let us see the selection."

The shop owner showed a select few of the most expensive rings. Liz chose two rings – one with diamonds for her and a simple design for Arun. The diamond ring was GBP 800 and the other one was GBP 600.

Chris remarked, "Arun's ring is simple but seems to be of excellent quality."

The shop owner said that the ring had been made in India, as it was of 22-carat gold. In India, jewelry is rarely of 18 or 19 carats as in Western countries. Chris was thrilled with the design and the selection. Liz was happy that Chris approved her choice and asked the shop owner to pack it. Liz filled out the amount in one of the signed cheques and gave it to the owner. He then gave Liz the packages, small as they were, and asked her to be very careful about theft and to put them in a safe deposit vault if they had one in the house. Liz thanked him for the advice. She would never have thought of that aspect of security even in the house. She placed them securely in her handbag, and they left the shop.

"Liz, we still have time, and we are right outside our favorite ice cream shop."

They entered the shop and ordered their choice of ice-creams with chocolate and nuts sprinkled on the top.

Chris said, "Liz, you are moving like a runaway train but heading to a safe destination and not into a crash. You have decided to make Arun your life-partner. I am envious of that only because you have found your soulmate – mine is nowhere in sight!

Liz smiled, "I am madly in love with him, and I know I have to act quickly; otherwise, with his shyness and cultural inhibitions, he will not make a move for another 2-3 years! Total seduction was my strategy, and he was more than a willing party – which makes me think that all that talk of culture, respect, etc., is based more on lack of opportunity."

Chris said, "I don't agree with you there. As a good-looking medic, many nurses would have queued up for him, not counting women doctors and consultants. His cultural values preserved him for YOU. So be thankful for that. He must have been a willing partner because he must also have recognized a soulmate in you."

"Yes, of course. I did not think of the previous situations in London, where he worked. You are right, Chris, that he must have avoided those approaches, and I'm glad he waited for me. Still, I did not realize that he would allow me to decide quickly on so many things, including marriage."

"What were the issues regarding marriage that were troubling him?"

Liz confided, "He mentioned that mum and dad and granddad might not agree wholeheartedly I may be cut off from my inheritance and excluded from the family home. He wanted to know how I would feel?"

Chris said thoughtfully, "Very pertinent points and let us tackle this one by one. What did you reply to his statement about losing your inheritance?"

"I told him that if my job were safe for life, so would my income, and I wouldn't need parental wealth. Also, that as I was mad for him to be my life partner, I would gladly give it up, and you could have the lot. He was very pleased with that reply. I can tell you!"

"Sis, I will not touch a penny of it, if they do that to you. If Arun gives me that job for life and a salary, then I too do not need parental support, and I will gladly take your side over theirs. You can count me in on that. Now, what of his observations about mum, dad, and granddad?"

Liz said, "He said that mum was more aggressive with me than with you and wanted to know why. Also, that dad was not showing any interest in the Surgery, although he never objected to us working there. At least there is passive support from him. Granddad, he feels, is an unknown material in that he talks nicely. Still, Arun suspects that he's stealthily trying to find out what the surgery revenue is when he is not required to do the accounts and opening cabinets he is not supposed to deal with."

"I agree with his sharp analysis and thorough evaluation of the three. I am also not sure about mum unless there are some secrets which we may not know now. Maybe Grandma knows, and I will try to find out. Dad, of course, is always laid back and happy to do nothing after spending his younger years amassing wealth. He deserves to put his feet up, and that is what he is doing. Grandpa, also I am not sure about, but he was always a cagey character with shifty eyes."

Liz said, "Arun also suggested that I still had a lot to learn about his background. You know, Chris, the driving time to hospital and back with him gives us time to talk about many issues."

Chris concurred, "Of course, the more you know about his background here and in India, the better. Fill me in on your discussions with him later."

Liz paid the bill, and they rushed back to rejoin the rest of the family.

Barbara asked, "Did you two buy anything at all? You don't seem to have any shopping bags with you."

Liz: said, "It was purely window shopping, mum. After a few minutes, we went to a café and had some nice chocolate ice cream."

"At least money saved!"

They returned to the hospital by 5:00 PM. Arun was far from finished, so Liz saw the others off and returned to wait for him in the office room.

CHAPTER 18

Seductions and Racism

Liz had about 90 minutes to wait, and she sat down in his comfortable chair, with its raised back. She sat thinking over the events of the last few days that had overturned her world. Like a tornado, she too had changed his life forever.

She remembered a limerick from her high school days:

There was a girl in Siam,
Who said to her lover, Khayyam -
To seduce me, you will have to use force,
Thank God you are Stronger than I am!

She could not resist a giggle. She did not know then that Arun had fallen in love with her from the moment he met her. Her corrosive words had slid past him, so taken had he been with her beauty. He had a vested interest in giving her the job she wanted and, at the same time, winning her family over. Spending long hours together and letting her see him best, as a professional, had worked its magic.

When she stood in front of him in the transparent negligee and slipped in under the sheets, he was quite ready and willing to be seduced. The next morning, he had run his hand over her sleeping body gently. She was half asleep and had assured him with a smile that all the goodies that he had enjoyed the previous night were in their right places, safe for more!

He had been in London for several years and was sought after by many women – nurses and doctors. He had never got attracted to any of them. He rarely went to parties so that he did not have to hold a girl to dance. He spent those hours studying procedures for his practice. He wanted to make money, lots of money, and help the community in whatever way he could. That was his path. But when he saw Liz, it was love at first sight – totally one-sided, not knowing how she would feel and whether she would reciprocate. He was also acutely aware of his color, and in the UK, those days, they tacitly practiced racism and apartheid in their own way. At least some of them did. Most of the people he dealt with were not that bad; they were overtly friendly and courteous.

If he had to put on his overcoat in the tube before getting down, any English man would hold his coat to slip his hands through. When he did not have a car, one of the white doctors or nurses would offer him a lift in theirs. Some had even waited for him till he finished his chores, to drive him back. He was always invited to Christmas lunches or pre-Christmas dinners when his colleagues realized he did not have any family here and was alone. If anyone made racist comments, his colleagues made sure the person apologized and left. Even in his own country, India, while living in Calcutta, the locals would ridicule him as he was from South India – Madras. Regionalism had led to many racist type comments in India itself.

In England, Lords and nobles had exploited the peasants for centuries, just as the upper castes had done in India. It was challenging to get any accommodation as many landlords would have boards outside their houses 'No vacancy for coloreds, but pets allowed.' At that time, there were no rules to prohibit such advertising. Many tacitly agreed with those sentiments.

A friend of his had been walking in a small village near London, when an old lady over 70 years of age, had waved her walking stick at him, motioning him to walk on the road as the pavement was for 'whites only.'

On the other hand, when he had gone to Southall, an area taken over by Sikhs from India, he had gone into an Indian store to shop. When he wanted to know the price of an item, he had to speak in Hindi as they did not speak or understand English. It was also an area where lampposts displayed signs like 'No spitting allowed.' In the subcontinent, sanitation standards were low, but in the UK, they had to resort to such signs in specific Asian areas.

His friend, from India, a student, had to spend a night in Bradford, amongst a predominantly Muslim area filled with Pakistanis. He saw a vacancy board at a B&B. On enquiring about staying for a night, he had to confirm whether he was a Pakistani or Indian. When he replied he was an Indian, they said that there was no vacancy. Arun had told Liz this to show that racism existed within the Asian community itself.

So, growing up in India in a way made one immune to some types of racist comments. The main difference is that in India, no one gave a thought to it being politically incorrect. Here, in the UK, they had started to stress about not using terms like colored or racist remarks. They had begun to refer to all brown-skinned people as 'Paki' from Pakistan, even though the subcontinent was composed of India, Pakistan, and Ceylon.

Liz thought of all these and understood why Arun was more tolerant of her comments, even when she told him to go back to his country and drive bullock carts. Being a physician, too, helped shield him from many adverse remarks, and his specialization in ophthalmology had won the admiration and gratitude of many patients. Many had thought that he graduated in the UK intending to go back to India but were surprised to hear that it was the other way around. He studied in India and then came to the UK to settle down.

She then thought about the marriage issues he had foreseen. It may work out all right for them, but their offspring might bear the effect of being mixed-race.

She had thought that Arun might treat this as a one-night stand with a white girl. But she was aware that he had told all of them that his life partner would be for life and that she would be the only one to have any relationship. He had also spoken about not having had any previous relationships in India or the UK. He was not the type to take advantage of a woman, and that too, of an employee.

Liz went to the observation room to see how the operations were going on and found no one in the theatre. So, she rushed back to the office to see Arun. He kissed her passionately and said it had been a good day with eight successful operations completed. These patients would check them tomorrow and signed the release notes. He said he was starving and needed to have something to eat soon.

"I will take you to the bakery for doughnuts or a small piece of cake."

"Sounds brilliant. Let's go."

They left for the shop, and she got him a doughnut and a small slice of cake.

Then they left for home.

Liz said, "We had a good shopping spree today, thanks to your money and cheques."

"Please treat this as our money from now on, and in the future, you can write your cheques. I have asked the Bank Manager to drop-in forms to make you a joint signatory to my account."

"Even before we are married?"

"Why not? Is it not imminent? Are you having doubts?"

Liz beamed, "I have no doubts. I like the idea of a wedding in the church in ordinary clothes, not to attract attention, with only Chris, Grandma, Bank Manager, Dave, Sally, Dick, and his wife. You and Chris could leave under the pretext of making a home visit to see a patient, and I can pretend to go with Gran for shopping. Mum and Granddad can stay in the surgery or return home like they usually do."

Arun: said, "I prefer the village church and do talk to the priest to ensure full secrecy. Request him also to make the service short. The Registrar should be on hand for us to fill the forms for the civil wedding. Ask Sally to organize the bouquet and flowers for the occasion. The church should be closed for all outsiders during the wedding service."

"Aye, Aye, Sir!" Liz gave him a mock salute, "I might arrange this on Wednesday, as you do not have any operations scheduled."

"What about the rings?" Arun asked. "I should have told you to buy them today itself. Will you be able to get them before Wednesday?"

Liz smiled, "Darling, I have already bought two rings; the diamond one is from you to me, and the plain band is from me to you. I took your ring for size. Please look into my bag and open the packet carefully."

He saw both the rings and was very impressed.

"You are due for some rewards, but I can't while you are driving."

"I will take a rain check for later," Liz smiled.

"Was Chris with you?"

"Chris was with me, and she loved it. She promised to keep the wedding news a secret. She will prepare Grandma for the news and the wedding. She too wants a life partner like you."

She pulled up outside the surgery, and they went in. They both went to Arun's room, and he grabbed her and kissed her urgently, and she responded equally fervently. They both stripped quickly and had an enjoyable 30 minutes of adult fun. Then they showered together, dressed, and left for her parents' place for dinner.

At dinner, the conversation focused initially on their admiration for Arun's skill in the delicate operations; then, they talked about the purchases and the delivery of the furniture. Barbara complained that the furniture was too expensive, but no one paid attention to her comments! All of them had enjoyed the shopping expedition and lunch out. They also admired Liz's dedication in wanting to be with Arun and lunching with him only.

After dinner, Liz, Chris, and Jessica went to the garden and entered the conservatory at Liz's request. Once inside, Liz closed the door and told them about her infatuation with Arun and how he felt the same way. Their wedding would take place the following Wednesday afternoon if the priest were agreeable. Liz did not want to have any issues with the 'color' of the bridegroom in the eyes of her mother, father, and granddad, and that is why she did not want them to attend. Grandma was surprised and thrilled and hugged Liz and assured her she would not breathe a word to others. She also understood and agreed with Liz's reticence in inviting others.

Jessica cautioned Liz in that any church wedding would need advance notice of the parties involved in the wedding, and it would no longer be a secret wedding. She advised them to get the Registrar in the Town Council to officiate the wedding.

Liz hugged her Gran and said she would pass on her suggestions to Arun.

Chris was thrilled about the quickness of the wedding. Liz said they should all be in plain working clothes; Sally would bring the flowers to the Registry Office discreetly. Liz told them not to look so pleased as others might want to know what happened. So, they went around the garden, pretending to look at all the flowers and plucking a few to put in a vase.

Liz and Arun left soon after. In Arun's room, Liz said, "I have told Grandma and Chris about the wedding date and to keep it a secret. Grandma was delighted, and even she agreed that it was best to keep the other three in the dark. She said we had her full support. She suggested a Registry Office, not a church wedding, so I will not talk to the priest."

"Nice piece of work, your grandma is a great character. One day I would like to know more about your family, and similarly, you all should know more about my background."

"Agreed, sir! Now, can we continue where we left off last night?'"

It would suffice to say they had another fantastic night of pleasure, followed by sound sleep.

CHAPTER 19

Bank Holiday Preparations

The next morning, they both left at 7.30 AM and reached the hospital by 8.00 AM. On the way Arun said, "Liz, sorry I didn't think of it earlier, but we should go to the Registrar's Office in the Town when we go to the hospital and request them for a Wednesday wedding.

"Good idea. I will find out and fill the form today."

She left him in the hospital after checking that all was set for the day and left for the Registry Office.

She then told him about the whole plan for the wedding and the date and time availability. The Registrar agreed to the following Wednesday at 3:00 PM and asked her to get the forms filled and submitted in a couple of hours.

The charge was under GBP 5.

Liz then returned to the hospital around 10:00 AM and got the form signed by Arun. She left for the Registry Office to apply. Liz came back to the hospital and had an hour or so to wait for Arun. She went into the office and locked the door – more for safety, as she found some of the consultants could be a nuisance. Liz wished Arun would come in during operations. She was impatient to tell him of this morning's progress.

Arun knew that Liz would lock the door, as she was uncomfortable with the consultant trying to make a pass at her.

As she feared, there was a knock on the door, and she knew it could not be Arun. She kept quiet. The knocking got louder and more insistent. So, she called security and told the guard that she was in Dr. Ayer's office, and he was to come at once. When she heard the guard was talking to someone outside, she opened the door and saw the most obnoxious consultant. The consultant said he was only trying to have a chat with her. The guard intervened and asked why he was banging the door. The consultant denied doing it and threatened the guard that he would see that the guard punished for telling lies.

"Doctor, you are obnoxious," she said vehemently, "I do not want to talk to you ever and do not try to come and chat me up when Dr. Ayer is not with me. I am going to make an official written complaint to Personnel Department (PD) about you and how you behaved."

The consultant got worried and, after apologizing to Liz and the guard, very sheepishly left the area. When Arun came, Liz gave him the details and had the guard corroborate her story. Arun took a complaint form and made Liz narrate the incident, blow by blow, and sign it. In another form, he got the guard to do the same. Then, he wrote a strongly worded letter urging the PD to take action against the offending physician.

This unpleasant incident clouded the return journey. Meanwhile, all the arrangements were in place. Dick and his wife were to come to the Registry Office by 2.30 PM on Wednesday. Arun agreed to do that. They went to the surgery, cleaned up, and went to Liz's home for dinner.

After dinner, they started discussing bank holiday preparations. Stephen said, "All the fliers given to all the village residents and the Small Town. It included the questionnaires as well. So, Liz and Chris's work will be lighter on the day."

Chris said, "We wait for you, Arun, to reveal your master plan."

Liz intervened, "Shouldn't we wait for the feedback from the questionnaires before pressing Arun for his plans? Let us discuss other items of importance."

Stephen said, "I agree with you, Liz. The food arrangements are complete, I understand. There will be a short speech by me around 4:00 PM for ten minutes. Arun will then address the gathering about his plans, and how the Village Committee can assist. Finally, the vote of thanks by Jessica."

Liz said, "Once we collate the details from the questionnaires, we can then set priorities for the way forward. We all are excited and Chris, more so than most, to see Mr. Robert Smith, if he turns up on Bank Holiday Monday."

"So, no details of the plan tonight," Chris said. "Well, tell us about your day."

Liz then narrated the trauma she suffered from the jerk of a consultant and the quick and decisive action they had taken immediately after. "We will have to wait and see how the hospital will respond," she concluded.

Barbara snorted, "These young doctors who misbehave are worse than immature adolescents. Don't the hospitals have a Code of Conduct spelling out the 'Do's and Don'ts' of proper behavior with women staff and colleagues? People like that should not be allowed to practice."

Arun said, "Practices and procedures are there, but the problem lies with lack of application and consistent follow-up. Some are more special than others, and so a few consultants can sometimes get away with murder. I am sure they will take some serious action in this case, which we will know about later in the week."

Stephen went back to the arrangements in the park. He said that putting up the marquee and related facilities were going as per plan and would be ready in good time. He wanted to know about a proposed visit by NHS representatives.

Arun: smiled, "I wanted to keep it a surprise. Since you brought it up, a team of five is coming to meet the Village residents and get their feedback. They usually take six months to report on the feedback but, as a special circumstance, will be visiting us in two months. They will come on Monday by 11:00 AM and leave by 4:00 PM."

Stephen patted him on the back, "I am sure we all appreciate their coming. It gives us an extra incentive to do things nicely to showcase the capabilities of the small Village and its committee."

Jessica said, "It appears all set for a wonderful bank holiday event, and I look forward to it with great enthusiasm this year because of Arun's involvement and contributions."

Later that night, when they were in bed, Liz confessed that she had been frightened when the consultant had banged the door, and she was grateful that she had the presence of mind to lock the door in the first place. "Arun, please do not leave me alone. I belong to you and you only," she whimpered. Arun held her close until she calmed down.

Arun whispered comfortingly, "Oh, Liz, it's only for a short while. Eventually, I will be moving my entire practice to the Village. I'm getting the bungalow converted for that. Till then, we'll have to take whatever precautions we can to keep you safe."

"Many thanks for thinking of me and protecting me. For the moment, I am happy with secure entry to the office. Also, strict instructions to the young doctors and consultants to mind their own business from the hospital's PD department will be appreciated."

On Tuesday, Liz asked Sally to order a simple floral arrangement so that the florist did not suspect that the flowers were for a wedding. She ordered them separately as if they were for different people and not for one customer. Sally said she would take the flowers to her house and then take it to the Registry Office along with cake, biscuits, and some wine on Wednesday, by 2.30 PM.

On Tuesday evening, Arun and Liz went through the plans for the Wednesday wedding. Chris and Dave would bring the rings just before the wedding to give to the Registrar. Sally was requested to arrange snacks in the adjacent hall for all to partake after the civil marriage. Tea and coffee with biscuits would also be provided, along with a celebratory bottle of champagne.

Liz then said, "Arun, let us celebrate tonight as this is our last night of 'living in sin.' From tomorrow afternoon, we are morally allowed to cohabit and consummate the marriage."

Arun laughed and said, "When do you think we should announce it to your parents? Also, what about the rings? When they see us wearing them, they will surely ask questions."

"I thought of that already. For a few days, at least, my solution is that I wear my ring when I go out shopping, visiting, socializing, or, more importantly, to the hospital. But you do not have to wear your ring. I can always claim that my ring is more to stop idiotic men from flirting with me."

"Liz, I feel that men will try to flirt with you, ring or no ring! Still, it's a splendid idea. But what will you reply if people then ask you who your husband is?"

Liz shrugged, "I will say that Dr. Ayer is my husband, and no one will say anything in the hospital. I'm sure they think we are knocking off together anyway!"

"I guess we'll have to take is as it comes."

Liz cuddled closer to the Arun, and soon they were lost to the world.

CHAPTER 20

First day of Reckoning

It felt like Charles Dickens' describing in his opening to *A Tale of Two Cities*. It was the best in the mornings. It was the worst of the mornings; it was the best of a day, it was the worst of a day. Worst because of all the worries about her parent's objections and consequences. These thoughts clouded their happiness. They had planned for Wednesday morning to be on a light schedule for Arun with the clinic starting only at 10:30 AM. Liz asked Sally to bring their breakfast early so that she could leave to sort out the flowers, snacks, etc. They finished their breakfast quickly, and Sally took their plates and cups away.

Arun was very reflective, and Liz could sense that. "What is bugging you, Arun? Are you getting cold feet?"

Arun hugged her tightly and said, "No, darling, I'm sad about not telling your parents and grandpa. Born of rich and loving parents, you must have dreamed of this day very differently, and I'm sure they too will be disappointed. I am sure you must be missing them too."

"Of course, I miss my parents. But I wanted to choose the person I want as a life- partner myself, and that person is you. For years my parents branded me as 'racist' for my many ill-judged comments and pressured me to change. Now I find that they are the ones with deeply held prejudices all along. It is better to have a few people at the wedding who wish us well, than a hundred hypocrites, even if some of them are your parents. I have no regrets, Arun. I will walk tall with my MAN and gladly wed YOU. I will happily be yours for the rest of my life."

"I feel the same way about marrying you. Still, I wish you would not harbor such bad feelings about your parents.

Liz, when it comes to race and color, there are many layers of behavior and different levels of acceptance. The transition is not seamless. It involves people, which includes all kinds of complex, conflicting emotions – dislikes, hatred, prejudice, and contempt, to name a few. There are a lot of areas where people of color are not welcome in a white society. Your parents can accept me as a physician but not as an intimate family member. Why, even in India, people are against inter-caste marriages, Hindus disapprove of marrying Muslims or people of any other religion or even caste, and vice versa. White people are not unique in this aspect.

People are like mirrors; when you smile at them, most will smile back at you; dislike them, and they will hate you as well. These are evident in day-to-day dealings with people.

Consequently, for your parents, it goes against the grain to accept that their much-beloved daughter is choosing to marry a man of color. So please be generous in your acceptance of them. I'm glad we have cleared the air; there are no more apprehensions in my mind."

Liz sighed, "You are right. I shall be as generous and patient with them as you were with me in the dark days of my racism. If they still disapprove of me and cut me off without a cent, then so be it! I hope you are not concerned that I might end up as a destitute without any money of my own?"

"Liz, if you knew about my background, you will not be asking me that question. You may even have serious doubts about marrying me."

"What is so bad about your background that is going to make me cancel the wedding in the last hour? You said you did not have any prior relationships with the opposite sex and that you did not even kiss till you kissed me. I hope all that is true?"

Arun shook his head, "Everything I've told you about my relationship with girls and kissing, is right. I will also never worry about you being destitute.

I am surprised you did not see the wedding application form after I filled in my details. I had to fill in as an Orphan under parental names.

Back in India, in Madras, I was an orphan, left outside an orphanage a few hours after my birth. The head of the orphanage, Mr. Shiva Iyer, said he saw a couple leaving a bundle at the gate and running away. He did not have the heart to get some youngsters to chase them as they may have had several reasons to make the difficult decision to give up their newborn.

Most of the orphanage children were acquired this way. I grew up there in the depths of poverty. But God was great in that I did well in studies, got scholarships, went to college, and studied medicine. No one else was of my mold. I do send GBP 200 every month to the orphanage to take care of 200 children residing there. I'll tell you more about that part of my life later.

I have experienced abject poverty. I don't expect anyone to come with a fortune. I have a very soft corner for people from poor backgrounds."

Liz looked at him with softened eyes, "You amaze me, my Darling. The wedding still goes ahead with this 'rags to riches' husband of mine. We will go to India, as you said before, to see the orphanage and the way of life you used to lead. Hey! Let's have one round of 'living in sin' before people start coming to the Surgery."

Arun obliged willingly.

When they went down together, there were naughty glances from Chris, but Liz pretended to be checking some papers for Arun. Chris followed Liz to her office and wanted an explanation for her being so late. Liz narrated the conversations she had with Arun, his background as an orphan in Madras, India, and how much struggle he had to go through to become a medical doctor.

Chris said: "Mum and dad won't exclude you from the inheritance. If that ever happens, I will voluntarily renounce my share as well and leave the house. That is my promise to you, and that is my conditional wedding gift to you both. You may never have to open the gift because things may not come to that stage, but if it does, then the gift is yours."

Liz embraced her sister with tears in her eyes and gave her a peck on both cheeks.

Chris commented, "Strange, these days, I do not have to wipe my cheeks after you kiss me, because you do not use lipstick these days, on doctor's orders!"

Liz smiled and ordered her sister to get on with her work and see to the patients.

There were a couple of emergency patients: mothers bringing in toddlers with a fever or a cough; Chris saw them after Arun had seen them first. By mid-day, the surgery was empty. Jessica told Stephen that she wanted to go shopping with Chris, and she would see him later that evening. Stephen left with Barbara. Sally and Dave had already left, so there were only four people in the surgery. They all heaved a sigh of relief. Sally had prepared some lunch for the four in the morning, a cold buffet with sliced meat and cake to follow. They had lunch in peace and talked about the afternoon.

By 1:00 PM, they decided to go their ways. Arun and Liz were to be in the next town before 2:30 PM, and Chris and Jessica were to get there separately. Dave and Sally with flowers and cake, drinks, etc. went separately to the Registrar's Office.

Jessica gave Liz a huge hug and said not to worry about anything and that all would be well. Chris also gave her sister a big hug. Arun also received affectionate embraces from Jessica and Chris.

As planned, Arun and Liz came to the council offices by 2:30 PM.

Chris and Jessica entered the Registrar's Office then and took their positions along with Dave and Sally. Chris was next to the bride, ready with the ring. The Registrar started the proceedings promptly at 3:00 PM and the exchange of rings and the signing of the marriage certificate with Jessica and Chris as key witnesses followed. The Registrar pronounced Arun and Liz as 'Man and Wife,' They kissed in front of the others – a rare privilege afforded to the couple as a must in wedding protocol. They then moved to the adjacent hall, popped the champagne and cut the wedding cake while the guests showered them with confetti and expressed their congratulations.

Arun requested others to keep the wedding a secret until Liz informed the parents at an opportune moment. They all agreed to it and blessed the newlyweds. As initially agreed, they all left the Registry and went in separate cars. Jessica went to her house, whereas Chris left with Liz to go to the surgery. Arun went to the bank to open a new joint account.

Chris asked, "Liz, how do you feel now? Happy and excited or concerned about the mum and dad issue?"

"In one sense, ecstatic; in the other, a sense of unease about what may lie ahead with parents and community. One thing for sure, you will not be poking any more fun about Arun, and I am living in sin!!"

Chris laughed, "I am glad you brought the whole thing to a happy conclusion quickly. Mum and dad will come around in time. I sincerely hope they do."

She left, saying she would meet Liz and Arun by 6:00 PM at home for dinner.

Liz left for the surgery, and Arun came with the new cheque and passbooks and gave it to her. She tossed them aside and drew him close for a very passionate kiss. She said she had wanted to do this ever since she had become Mrs. Ayer. They went to the bedroom and taking out the bank stationery. She wrote the first cheque to Sally for GBP 20 as a big thank you for all the beautiful arrangements and food she had prepared. She enclosed the check inside a 'Thank You' card, which she had already bought to give Sally the following day.

Then, she and Arun undressed and enjoyed their first conjugal pleasure. When they woke up, it was time for a quick shower before they for Jeff and Barbara's home. They reached the house at 7:00 PM, and Arun apologized for the delay, making the excuse of urgent calls. Both Jessica and Chris grinned wickedly at this because they knew what exactly had delayed the newlyweds.

Dinner conversation once more focused on Bank Holiday Monday preparations.

Stephen reported, "Everything is on track. The local hotel in the next town has had a few bookings for the three days, and many B&B's in the village also took bookings. This year the bookings have been made much earlier and in larger numbers. I am happy about the whole arrangement."

Barbara added, "The questionnaires would be in the community hall after completion. Do you have any update on that, dad?

Stephen responded, "I mention to the Village community by circular and through word of mouth, that all the replies should be delivered by Friday so that Liz and Chris will have time to sort out the replies and list priorities by Saturday, for Arun to plan his talk for Monday. People from the small town nearby also wanted to participate, and we had to print out more forms for them to fill."

Barbara said, "Do you think the whole thing has gotten a lot bigger than we planned and might blow up in our faces?"

Stephen replied, "Not really because it is an honest attempt by Arun to find a strategy for community improvement. Anyway, let's see what happens on Monday."

Arun said, "Many thanks to you, Stephen and Barbara, for your inputs. I request you not to preempt what I want to say before Monday during discussions. Initially, I wanted to keep it a secret only known to Liz and Chris, as they will have a huge role to play. They are not aware of what they are getting themselves into yet, but I'm sure they will enjoy the commitment and the challenge their tasks will involve. However, now I feel we should all have a family discussion on Sunday night at home, a brief one."

Barbara said, "We will be glad to have a preview of what is to come on Monday."

Arun said, "Stephen, I would like to bring forward our plans by a day. Liz and Chris should have a team of 5-6 volunteers for the two age groups, up to 12 and 13-25 respectively, and distribute the questionnaires to them. Also, I have a survey for all visitors, which you and Jessica should distribute. All the results will be on the two notice boards. I will report on the results at the end of the meeting.

Stephen: said, "I like your proposed timeline. I will alert the Village Committee about these and how they should cooperate for the good of the village."

It was already 10:00 PM, and Liz and Arun returned to their Surgery and their bed.

Liz mused, "How strange! A few weeks ago, you were nobody to me, but now you are the only one for me and love it."

Arun said, "I feel the same way. I was very concerned whether I would ever meet you again, and now we are intrinsically bonded together for life. I will be counting on you, and you will be masterminding the changes for us. One day you will be very popular throughout the country for your unstinting community work. The issue is how to break the news to your parents and get that issue out of the way. I prefer that they hear it from us than through someone else's careless talk. We have to live in peace and harmony with them."

Liz sighed, "My concern about informing mum and dad is weighing on my mind constantly. I will find an opening and break it to her first while you are busy elsewhere."

"Are you concerned that they may say something harsh, and it is better I do not hear it? Well, I will leave it up to you to know the best strategy to deal with your parents."

Liz assured him, "There will be no secrets between us, and I will let you know all the details once we are snuggled up in the bed, as we are now."

Arun said thoughtfully, "I have a bad feeling about your granddad, but I cannot say why. Outwardly he seems so helpful, but I feel somehow, he is pursuing another agenda."

Liz confessed, "We have always felt that Grandma was our rock. Grandpa, we were never that close to him. Both Chris and I have felt uncomfortable around him but put up with him for Grandma's sake. Your suspicions may be right. Our house, in a way, is a mystery to Chris and me. Sometimes we feel a rich family has adopted us."

Arun said, "Darling, let us not close this special day with negative thoughts. We will have to take whatever comes up in our stride. For now, let's enjoy the first night after marriage. What we are missing out on is a pleasurable honeymoon. Let's try and make up for it, right here."

After several minutes of marital bliss, they slept in each other's embrace.

CHAPTER 21

Revelations

The preparations for the bank holiday were on full swing. The whole village was buzzing. But for a few, the extra buzz was due to the presence of Arun, the local GP. Those close to Arun knew what plans he had for the village, even though they were unaware of the details yet. Dave and a few of his mates were busy erecting the large marquee and building stalls. Sally and her friends were busy with external and internal decorations. Two months after the arrival of the local GP, the villagers were happier and healthier. There were fewer cases of common ailments like flu or cold due to the preventive measures that Arun advised each patient when they came to the Surgery. He also warned against strenuous exercises and demonstrated how to lift items, bend, etc., without straining their backs. Chris and Jessica also advised the women about keeping good health and eating wisely. The presence of a Health Visitor like Jessica had pleased the village women.

The GP in the small town nearby had left suddenly, and they could not find a replacement. The NHS authorities asked Arun for his advice, and he suggested that he operated evening surgeries in the small Town and morning surgeries in the Village. It meant that his entire staff had to work in the existing Surgery and the small Town. Dave did the modification to the Surgery facilities as stipulated by Arun. Arun also performed the clinics, between the two Surgeries – alternate weeks in each Surgery. That seemed to please the people of the small Town. He was always on call at other times, for the whole community, five days a week.

On Tuesday evening, during dinner, Stephen said, "Arun, I understand that a team of NHS top brass is coming to the village on Bank Holiday Monday, between 12:00-3:00 PM. I heard that they might be investigating a complaint against you and Liz."

Liz looked up, startled, "What have I done? Unless it related to that jerk, the young consultant who tried to misbehave with me."

Arun said, "I know that that young doctor's dad is in an influential position in the NHS, and he might be misusing his position and contacts to discredit us. How did you know of this, Stephen?"

Stephen shrugged, "My friend in BMA told me about this 'Trojan Horse' type of visit to the Village. So, beware and be prepared to be questioned."

Arun said, "Thank you, Stephen, for forewarning us. I did not mention it to anyone till now. I had received a letter from the NHS HQ about this visit and that it would be only a cosmetic investigation to please the funding businessman. However, there is one member who is a close buddy with the businessman, and he may cause some awkwardness. So, we must collect enough data and evidence from the people in the adjoining rooms in the hospital to corroborate our account."

Liz said, "I might drop you off and check on the furniture deliveries later this week. Dave has painted the downstairs in the color scheme I have chosen. He only needs to put the furniture in place. I am very pleased with his skillful work."

Arun smiled, "It is nice to know that the bungalow is being ready for you next week. I understand he will start on the 4-bedroom extension on the side after Bank Holiday Monday. You can drop me in the hospital and spend the rest of the day with your family."

Chris added, "We are all going to have a whale of a time tomorrow afternoon. You can be sure of that."

Barbara and Jessica were surprised to find out that their respective husbands would be accompanying them too. They decided to take the 8-seater van to the shops with Chris doing the driving.

When Liz and Arun returned to the house and were in bed, Liz said, "I do not like what I heard about the NHS visit. Are you worried too?"

"No, Liz, but it is an unnecessary irritant at this crucial time with our first Village get together. They will try to discredit you to find a way to let the consultant continue at the hospital. In the process, they might imply that you have been the one to lead him on, especially if this is his first offense. NHS does not want to face legal action for unlawful dismissal. They will be looking for a solution that does not cost them any money. So, be prepared for a roller coaster ride when they talk to you. I am trying to avoid that by gathering enough evidence to make a cast-iron case. I hired a private detective to check out any such incidents in the past, which led him to leave the other hospitals and eventually come to this one."

Liz frowned, "Will the NHS look kindly upon for you doing this type of investigation when you are an NHS employee?"

Arun said, "You are my PA, and paid from my private practice. So, I am defending my employee and my business. In any case sense, Liz, we should set up an ophthalmology clinic with 5-6 convalescence rooms to treat patients in the village. The operations done outside NHS premises bear no connection with the NHS in my business."

"At least then there will not be any young jerk making passes at me. I hope when the dust settles, you will put that project into operation."

Arun warned, "Also, Liz, I have a warning that someone might have complained about us being close and raised the race issue. I'm wondering who could have alerted the NHS to this. It has to be someone close to us who is trying to break us up. I have a feeling it is your granddad. I could be wrong. We will know for sure next week."

Liz looked up, alarmed, "I am shocked to hear that, and I cannot understand how you stay calm under this kind of pressure. I sincerely hope it is not granddad. But I respect your gut feelings on these issues."

"Let me find out more in the next couple of days. I'm sure they must be others who would have heard the doctor banging the door when you were inside the room in the hospital last Wednesday."

"Okay, Sherlock, I leave it to you. It may take a few years before I become your Dr. Watson! I am so worried. I need a good hug and want to lie in the safety of your tender embrace. Let us get on with our duties as a newly-wedded couple and then get some sleep."

The next day Liz removed her wedding ring and put it in her purse. After morning surgery, Arun and Liz left for the hospital with Chris and the rest of the family. Liz's dad and granddad followed in the van. When they arrived at the hospital, she put on her wedding ring and said it was for safety from predators. After she had dealt with the paperwork in the office, she went out with the others to a restaurant for lunch.

Barbara observed, "Liz, I see you wearing an expensive wedding ring. Are you trying to protect yourself by pretending you are already married?"

"Yes, mum, you are spot on."

If they ask you who your husband is, what are you planning to say? Arun?"

"Yes, mum, no better protection than being married to a Consultant in the hospital. That is the best insurance, don't you think?"

Barbara shrugged, "I suppose so."

Chris discreetly winked at Liz, encouraging her to take it further.

Liz drew a deep breath, "Mum, there's something I've got to tell you and dad, I am already married to Arun. I've been Mrs. Ayer, since last Wednesday afternoon. We got married discreetly. I am sorry for not inviting you both and granddad, because you may have objected and tried to stop us."

Barbara paled in shock. "What are you saying, Liz? You are married, and we did not know? We may have agreed, you know."

Liz smiled, "In which case, we will get married all over again, calling a lot of people as you would have liked."

Barbara sat slumped in shock, "You have driven a knife through my heart, Liz. I wanted to do so much for you, but you married Arun without consulting us. He is alright as a friend, but as a husband?" She shook her head, sorrowfully.

"Arun did try to warm me, mum. He told me that that there are many shades of acceptance between hating people of color and agreeing to treat them as equals, in a white society. Furthermore, he did warn me that to be a husband to a white girl might be too much for you to accept as parents. I accepted his honest sentiments but convinced him that I had chosen him as my life partner, and his race or color would not change my mind. He did ask me to think it over, but I refused. You know how I can be."

Barbara protested, "I appreciate his honesty, but knowing all that he still went ahead. He should have told us."

Liz drew herself up, "I am over 18, and by law, I do not need parental consent. He is a fine gentleman, and I feel blessed to have him as my husband."

Jeff: "I bless you both, but I am uneasy that your mum has been overlooked by not being informed or invited to the wedding."

Barbara rose to her feet, "After this humiliation, I have nothing to say other than you are no longer my daughter, and I request you not to come home anymore."

Liz pleaded, "Mum, please do not say words that you might regret. I'm not the first girl to marry without parental consent, and I will not be the last. Home is my dream house, and I know of no other place so important to me, and it's full of my childhood memories."

"You should have thought of all this before your hasty marriage. Now it is too late. You have always been a disappointment to me. I will see that you do not inherit any of our wealth. You are on your own. From now on, I have only one daughter, Chris."

Liz said with dignity, though her heart was breaking, "I am sorry you feel that way. Arun did warn me about my loss inheritance, and I was fully aware of it. I am more worried about the emotional loss of not being able to talk to my mum as girls do. Loss of money does not bother me as much as a loss of contact with you and dad."

Barbara was unrelenting. "I speak for dad as well. You have chosen your path; let us leave it at that."

Chris jumped in, "Mum, I knew you and dad might be upset, but cutting her off from the family? That's vindictive."

Barbara turned on her, "Chris, did you know about this wedding, and did you attend?"

Jessica said, "The wedding held in the Registry Office in town with only a few people before she could reply. Chris and I signed the marriage certificate as witnesses. When they asked me about telling you three, I agreed that a secret wedding would be best. Barbara, if you disown Liz, let me tell you that our family wealth has been handed down from the maternal side, thankfully. You do not have any legal right to exclude her from the wealth of the house where she grew up. Our grandparents had created the trust to protect the coming generation, and the house is part of the trust. You and I have no control over that. Your wealth can deny her, but not our ancestral wealth, nor can you ban her from coming to her house."

Chris said hotly, "I am glad Liz married Arun, a fine gentleman and a man of vision for the village. If you disown her as your daughter, then I will disown you both as my mum and dad, and I will not visit the house until you apologize to both of us. As Grandma says, you have no right over the ancestral property – your own, yes. I am sorry it had to come to this shoddy level of accusations and vengeance."

Liz sighed, "I do not know how to react now. I can leave here, and we will stop coming to the house anymore. I will tell my husband that dinner will be in the Surgery from now on, and we might have to get on with the Bank Holiday Monday event with the help of Chris and Grandma only, unless you change your mind in the interim. Also, it appears that both dad and grandpa have no opinion of their own."

Jessica said, "Stephen, Liz told me that someone has complained to NHS about her and Arun"

Stephen raised an eyebrow, "You don't suspect me of being the one to leak this information, surely?"

Jessica said, "If it turns out that you were the root cause, then I will expect you to leave our house and make your arrangements from now on. You will no longer get any money from me. I have put up with your devious ways in the past. As those incidents did not affect me, I turned a blind eye, but not this time. Arun is part of my family, and I will not allow anyone to discredit him, even if it happens to be my husband. I will not hesitate to divorce you. So please own up."

Stephen bristled, "I take exception to your comments."

Jessica warned, "You can do what you like. If you do not come clean now and later come to know you had a hand in it, then all I said will happen. Be aware of that."

Stephen spluttered, "I did speak to a few people about the concerns I had over Arun, but I did not expect them to complain, dear."

"Stephen, please do not 'dear' me. Please make arrangements to leave the house tomorrow morning. I will give you GBP 500 so that you can go to London or anywhere else or get you a ticket to Botswana, but it will only be a one-way ticket. What would you like?"

"One-way to Botswana, and that is the end of our relationship forever."

"Good riddance is my feeling. I am very relieved now. Liz and Chris, let us go to the travel agent and get a flight booked for tomorrow so that Stephen can leave this evening for London. From now on, Chris can stay with me, and we will have dinner at my house."

Liz said, "Grandma, will you and Chris, please have dinner with us tonight, and we will plan regular dinners in due course."

Jessica patted her hand, "That's fine with me, Liz. Let us leave the car with Barbara, and we'll take a taxi. Stephen, you better have your case packed once and for all. If I cannot get a ticket for tomorrow, you can stay with Barbara until you leave for London."

Stephen hissed, "I have no more interest in you or the Village, and I hope you get a ticket for tomorrow. I will come with you to the travel agent right now."

The grandparents, Chris and Liz, went to the travel agent and were lucky to get one ticket for Gaborone, the capital of Botswana, the next day from London. By 5:00 PM, Stephen had packed and left the Village for good. Chris, Liz, and Jessica went to the hospital and waited for Arun to finish all his operations. He came out by 5:00 PM. They met in the office, and Liz briefed him on the afternoon's incidents and how things had turned out as he had predicted.

"You were right once again, Arun. My mum disowned me and tried to deny me my inheritance. Luckily Grandma stepped in. Chris also told mum that she would disown them due to treating me so shabbily. It was a shame we parted like this. So, we have to manage the Bank Holiday Monday events. Also, you were right in suspecting granddad.

He owned up after Grandma threatened him. He now has a one-way ticket to Botswana. He has gone from us for good. Chris will be staying with Grandma from tonight."

Arun sighed, "I am so sorry about this unpleasantness. Something tells me that your mum will change her mind once the initial shock has worn off. Her mother and daughters disowning her and her dad leaving the UK for good…" he shook his head remorsefully. " It is sad. I am sure once she mulls over the day's events and her contribution to the crisis, she will regret it. Tomorrow is another day, so lets us not lose hope."

Liz asked, "How did you get on with your fact-finding on the young consultant?"

"Some people have given written reports that they heard the banging and saw him doing it. They also reported that he threatened the security guard with dismissal. Personnel Department (PD) has written a strong report as well, which the NHS has received. Based on it, NHS informed PD that the young doctor would be transferred to London and face 'fitness to practice' charges. So, it looks like we will have one less set of inquisitions to worry about on Monday. We can focus on our projects for the Village with a free mind."

Liz said, "I do not know how you are so calm when a storm has blown."

"There is always a calm after the storm. I hope everything will be cleared up by this evening, if not, definitely by tomorrow."

They reached the Surgery at 5:30 PM and were surprised to see Barbara's car parked outside. They entered the Surgery and went to the reception. Barbara was crying, and as soon as she saw Liz, she gave her a big hug and said sorry a million times for the words she had said to her. She then hugged Arun and said,

"I am very pleased that you have become my son-in-law. I have said several disturbing things to Liz, but I ask forgiveness from all of you."

Arun said, "You are like a mother to me. You never have to apologize for what a mum says to a daughter or son out of anger. It was all done in a highly charged, emotional, and even irrational moment, and it is better to put it aside. I am glad you had the courage and humility to come and apologize to your daughters – that took some taking. I applaud you for that."

Barbara said, "Out of anger, I asked Liz not to come to the house. It is her house, and she can come and go whenever she wants. I will never stop her. I would like you all to come home for dinner. Also, from now on, dinner will be at our place only. Mother, Chris, I want you both to stay in the house with me. I cannot stay there on my own."

Jessica asked, "Why on your own, Barbara?"

"For some weeks, Jeff has been restless, especially with all of us working at the Surgery. He wanted to go back to South Africa. Jeff asked me to get him a one-way ticket to South Africa. He packed his case, and he and Stephen both caught the train to London. After dropping them off, I came and sat here thinking. What cruel words I uttered that caused this total devastation in our family. My dad and Jeff had a different plan and never quite got on with us. It was a life of pretense. Now it came to light, and I am glad it turned out this way. Mum, I want you to come and stay with me forever, and we five will live happily from now on. I don't want you to be living in Surgery anymore. Use those as consulting rooms, the same with the bungalow extension. You both are not staying there when your own house is down the lane."

Jessica said, "Arun, your prophecy has come true. We all should take up the offer from Barbara and live there together. Arun, from now on, you are the man of the house."

Arun smiled, "What can I say, let me pack my suitcase immediately."

Barbara said, "Arun, please wear your wedding ring, and I'd like to see both your rings now. Liz, your ring is stunning. When did you buy it?"

Liz giggled, "Chris and I went shopping after choosing the furniture and selected the rings."

"It is always the mum who hears about it at the very last. I hope it will not be like that from now on."

Liz and Chris hugged her fondly and said a sea change had taken place in all their attitudes for the better, and she would tell her all little details, even insignificant ones! Barbara had a good look at the rings and gave it back to them to wear.

"My wedding presents to both of you is to stay in the house forever, and all costs of living will be mine – or more accurately, paid by the Trust Fund."

Arun and Liz were touched by her generosity and hugged her. There were tears in everyone's eyes. Then Liz and Arun packed their cases for the next three days and planned to take the rest of their clothing and other personal items the following day. By 7:00 PM, they were in their new house.

They had a quiet dinner, and the presence of dad and grandpa was missed, of course. But Barbara and Jessica seemed relieved at their newfound freedom. They had now got a cast-iron family unit to spend the rest of their time together.

Barbara told Arun, "I need to tell you about our family history, which was kept a secret from both my daughters. But it will not be so from today. Let the long weekend finish, and we will sit down, open the family cupboards, and reveal all the skeletons."

Arun said, "I have a large skeleton in my cupboard, which I revealed to Liz on the day of the wedding, in case she wanted to back off. Fortunately, she didn't. If she had, then I may have died of a broken heart. I read somewhere that 'When the skin of the human body – 80% water – is cut, blood comes out. But when our heart – full of blood – is cut, only water comes out as tears. Such is the unique relationship between water and blood for all humans.' I will also tell you my side of the story at that time, not now."

Jessica: "I have my skeletons too; most of Stephens' over the years before and after Barbara was born. I have not told her all of her dad's despicable deeds. I will also reveal it all and clear my chest of bad memories once and for all."

Liz said, "You know, Arun told me within a few days of meeting us that there was something wrong with three members of our family – mum, dad, and granddad. He is so sensitive and correct in his assessment. Until he mentioned it to me, I had not noticed it, but it became apparent to me when he pointed out. I am interested in listening to you all. Even though Arun has told me his background in a gist, I hope to hear the blow-by-blow account soon."

Chris laughed, "Your miserable lot, why not tell us today as I cannot sleep until I have heard it all! Okay, with great reluctance, I will wait with bated breath I look forward to the day of revelation."

They all laughed and then retired to bed. Arun had not seen Liz's bedroom here before. Her room was huge, twice the size of the Surgery. Plenty of cupboard space – he wondered how women could fill all the area and want more! She promised to vacate a wardrobe for him later that week. Then they brushed their teeth and got into bed.

Liz said, "I'm so happy mum came around so quickly. It was also nice of her to let us stay here permanently. Mum is always mum despite harsh words spoken in anger. I had misunderstood her all these years, and I am ashamed of it. Don't you think so, Arun?"

Arun said, "I agree with the first part about the misunderstanding. I cannot comment on the second part, as I have had no previous experience of having a mother. All children with mums should be grateful for being blessed with them and try to understand and even put up with the pain even on hearing harsh words. I am sure Liz you will be a much better person for dealing with your mum. I am glad you can live with your mother. Money is not everything. We will have plenty without the fund. But the emotional bond with a mum is difficult to get and has to come from mum only."

"Arun, you have a wonderful way with words. Without further ado, we need to consummate the marriage in our new home, don't you think?"

Arun laughed and obliged her and took her to a different world of bliss. They slept well that night – fulfilled not only physically, but emotionally too.

CHAPTER 22

Promised Land

When Liz woke up, she realized she had to drive to the Surgery, as they no longer lived above it. She woke up Arun, and they rushed to get ready. They reached the Surgery by 8:15 AM. Liz told Sally that she and the doctor would be sleeping in her house and not in Surgery. She also said her mum, dad, and granddad knew about the wedding and that all was well. Dinner would be at the house every day. Instead, Sally could take over the cooking of lunch in the Surgery for all five of them. She agreed, and Liz told her that her parents had accepted the marriage quite well.

On Thursday, everyone was busy at the Surgery, and there was hardly any time to focus on the work scheduled for the weekend. Liz had been to the community hall in the Village to check on volunteers to assist her and Chris. She said that a notice would be put up on the board, the next morning, in the community hall.

Arun said, "I am pleased that you had a good turnout for willing volunteers. I had a call from the NHS board about taking over the small Surgery in Town next to us. They fear no one will turn up, and the residents may not have a GP for the next 2-3 years. They have accepted my proposal for alternating surgery work between the Village and the Town, and they discussed payments based on the size of the population, as is the norm. I am delighted with it."

Jessica asked, "Does it mean I will have to go there and back each day?"

Chris said, "Grandma, you can ride with me. One day we will work there and the next day here. The drive is only five miles, and I'll be driving you. It won't be tiring. I will be with you."

Arun continued, "I have put a new circular on the notice board in the Village hall calling for people to work in the Surgery as receptionists, nurses, clerical workers healthcare assistants, midwives, etc. I have also asked them to specify what they are good at and what they think they can do. Liz, can you allocate four volunteers to meet people coming to the marquee on Saturday and ask them to fill out the forms."

Liz said, "I'll do it and take the application forms for each posting from you later. It is going to be a hectic weekend for all of us."

Arun said: " Jessica, I would like your help in assessing the applicants for the midwife's position and Chris, I would like you to do the same for nurses. These are not selection interviews but to gauge their willingness to work in the Village or Town Surgery. I will do the final interviews next week."

Chris cut in, "If we are going to have two premises, and take in more staff, will you consider taking me on as a partner?"

Arun laughed at her, eagerness, "You are hoping so, aren't you? Continue your daily training for some time before we come to that bridge."

Barbara asked anxiously, "With so many new staff, being recruited, do you still need me in the surgery?"

Arun said, "Only you can decide whether you want to work or not. As for me, I will always encourage you to continue working until you drop. The same applies to Jessica as well."

Jessica smiled, "Many thanks for that, Arun. I love working with pregnant women and helping them at a crucial period in their lives."

They then had coffee and watched the news. Around 9:00 PM, Arun wanted to read an article from a medical journal.

Barbara said, "I will get the room next to your bedroom converted to an office for you and Liz to read in or work. It will be ready by tomorrow afternoon. You can use Chris's study for now."

"I would prefer to read the article in bed. I hope there are table lamps on both sides of the bed for people to read?"

Liz said, "Till now, I have been single while sleeping here. So, I will get a lamp fitted for you tomorrow. Today, you can sleep on my side of the bed and use my table lamp."

Chris promptly said, "What a gesture and sacrifice from you, Liz, for your hubby. You are the perfect Solomon to get a solution so quickly!"

Liz and others smiled at Chris' teasing.

Barbara said, "I am so happy that you all are here. Honestly, I do not miss my dad or my husband. It was always a strained relationship. I am sure the Village Committee will ask about the sudden departure of the two, but I will tell them that unforeseen business circumstances called for their urgent departure. I am sure they all know how much dad and Jeff love Botswana and South Africa."

Jessica: "Yes, I do, Barbara. Stephen was always friendly to all the ladies of the Village, and I put up with that for a long time. But recently, he started talking about blacks and their rule if whites lost the apartheid battle. He was the ringleader of the hate group, not you, Liz. They used you to mask Stephen's identity. He was the sweet talker in front of Arun, but when we came back home, he would say many nasty things about Indians. I tolerated it for a few days but could not stomach anymore. The last straw was when he told NHS representatives might question Arun about his relationship with a white girl – Liz. I told him then to get out of the house. He has never worked a single day in his life. It was all my dad's money and let me not start on the affairs he had with the black servants! For that, he didn't mind their color. For over 30 years, I have not allowed him into my bedroom for fear of getting venereal diseases.

After Barbara was born, he went to Botswana, and then his sexual activities started. When I heard about it, I confronted him, and he confessed. I told him that I would never sleep with him again. For the sake of society, we would remain husband and wife, but nothing else. I do not regret sending him packing him for good. I wish I had done so many years ago. There are no more skeletons in my cupboard.

However, Barbara was a wild kid, and she was so beautiful but kept the lousy company in Botswana. I never gave up on her, never said the kind of things she told you, Liz. My love for her was never conditional at any time. I used to cry at night, asking God to give her back to me safe and loving. Eventually, he did."

Liz stroked her hand, "Grandma, we are sad to hear of your bad luck with your husband, but what a brave face you put on in front of me and Chris and society. We never liked him hugging us, and we used to run away if you were not in the room or the house. We never told you all these years and would never have, had you had not been open with us about him and his weak character. We are also stunned to hear about mum, and will wait for her to tell us eventually,"

Chris: said: "I endorse what Liz said, Grandma. Granddad was not a nice person, and a grown-up girl had to be extremely careful around him."

Barbara gasped, "What a shocking revelation from you three! I never realized that so many undercurrents were there in our family. We appeared to be close-knit but were not so in reality. I think we should all talk about nicer things for the rest of the night."

The three understood that mum was not going to spill any beans that night. They chatted for a while about the snacks for the weekend functions. Then Liz yawned and said she would turn in.

Barbara said, "Mum, I heard what you said about me, and I'm sorry for troubling you in my teen years. In a way, I am so happy that Liz and her husband are with us and sleeping in the same house as us. I have never felt so happy in this house all these years until now. I will make sure that I never do or say anything to upset Liz again. Please, both of you correct me if I step out of line, however small an issue it might be."

Chris and Jessica agreed, and they went to bed to prepare for the busy next day.

Liz went to the Village hall to put up the notices and asked the selected volunteers to contact her ASAP. Mr. Fisher, the Treasurer for the Village Committee, asked where her granddad was. Liz said she had not seen him yet and slipped quietly. She knew Grandma would tackle the question much better than Chris or her.

During the day, the volunteers went about collecting all the questionnaires and separated them by age groups. Chris got the under-12's, and the 13-25 age group went to Liz. Arun gave his instructions, and all the volunteers left the Surgery to proceed with their tasks.

Arun had two important phone calls, one from the NHS HQ and one from the Hospital HR. He was pleased with both the calls and planned to tell the others about them later. By evening, out of 1600 questionnaires circulated, 960 had responded. The volunteers then audited these, and the resident's preferences for facilities in the Village were listed and given to Liz and Chris.

The work in the park was nearly complete. Marquee was ready, decorations placed inside along with furniture for the committee, and the rest of the people to sit on. All electrical lighting, mike systems, loudspeakers at various places around the park, and other minor work finished. All 16 stalls had been erected and furnished. In a nutshell, the functions could start that evening – so was the Village's preparedness for the weekend activities.

Jessica and Barbara went to the Village hall in the morning to let the Treasurer and others in the committee know the reasons for the absence of Stephen and Jeff. Jessica said they both had an urgent SOS from South Africa and Botswana, respectively, about mines in a dangerous state, and they could lose everything overnight. So, they had left on Wednesday evening for London. Their return under these conditions of political uncertainty was challenging to predict. The committee was sad to hear the news. But they were all used to hearing about the sudden change of fortunes of UK investors in Africa, and they wished Jessica and Barbara the best of British luck to hold on to their investments. The Treasurer, Mr. Fisher, said they would be able to manage the weekend arrangements without any problem.

Barbara admired teasingly, the way her mum had articulated and mapped out a plausible scenario. She said her mum was still the same old cunning fox of the yesteryears. They went back to the Surgery, and then all the family left for home.

During dinner, Arun announced, "I had two essential telephone calls and some splendid news.

The first news from NHS HQ was that the full committee of the hearing was not coming. They will send only one representative to see the Village Committee's participation and take on-the-spot views about the Surgery to date. They said that the hospital had sent them a stinging report about the young consultant, listing all his bad behavior. They have filed a complaint with the General Medical Council questioning the doctor's fitness to practice medicine.

The other good news is that the racial complaint about the close relationship between Liz and me was not an issue as the perpetrator had sent a letter of apology for writing a false accusation. He also seems to have confessed that he was the leader of the hate group in the Village for years but made it look like Liz was the leader. He assured them that the group had been dismantled for good for fear of legal action by the authorities, especially when the new GP was doing good work and was hugely popular with all. They did not tell me who the person was, but my guess is it is Stephen.

Therefore, only one representative will come with no particular agenda and will discuss with me the logistics of managing the Town Surgery, as well."

Liz burst out, "I am so relieved. I would not have withstood any questioning about our relationship. I am glad it is not a national issue anymore! Also, we are not getting famous for the wrong reasons!"

Barbara said, "Good news all around. I have to agree my first suspicion would fall on my dad. Only mum can confirm that."

Jessica said, "Arun, you are correct. I made him write that letter and post on the same day. He did not have an answer when I asked him why he involved Liz in his nefarious activities. Anyway, it is all over now, and we can start a new chapter."

The irrepressible Chris added, "Mum, we are indeed a mix of evil characters masquerading as a loving family all these years. But for your wealth, we would have been found out and been guests of Her Majesty's prison for life!"

Arun said, "Oh, and I forgot to say – the news from the hospital reinforced what NHS HQ told me verbally. They had a letter about the consultant sent to Australia on a new assignment. It seems they left out the bit that he had to leave."

Chris said dramatically, "Astonishing, Liz! The first man to make a pass at you loses his license and ends up down under! You should carry a warning sign, STAY AWAY; COME NEAR AT YOUR PERIL."

They were all amused by the remark. Arun asked Liz and Chris to work on the lists and select three items from each list as chosen by the parents. Arun, Liz, and Chris met at 8:30 PM to go over the priorities:

Under 12's: A primary and early secondary school; a kindergarten and a playground for very young children 3-6 with protective enclosures.

13-25 age group: They needed an excellent secondary school with lab facilities; football, cricket grounds, and tennis courts – outdoors and indoors; finally, a career training skill center for woodwork, electrical and mechanical trades, car mechanics, etc.

Arun said, "I am thrilled with the lists, and I think they are do-able. One needs a small investment in setting up the facility. We need a philanthropist to donate and a charity to raise funds for the village. We will have to seek help from the committee as well as approach some industrialists for funding."

Barbara had an idea. "I know the next-door property is for sale, and I was asked by its owner in South Africa to sell it at market value. I will telephone him after I get the valuation done by the estate agent. I am not sure who will come forward to put up the money, but that is the next step."

Arun: declared, "When there is a will for the people to do something good, then God will always show the way. Let us wait and see."

They all retired to their respective rooms. Liz said, "I am so happy the jerk is out of our lives when in bed. Because of your good work, good things happen to us. I need to reward you handsomely for this, don't you think?"

"Whatever the reason, I will gladly accept your rewards anytime, anywhere."

They slept very well that night.

Saturday dawned bright and sunny – the kind of day described by the British Press as "Indian summer." People strolled around, enjoying the stalls and the various snacks. They gathered in the marquee again around 2:00 PM, when the Village Committee occupied the stage, and Arun made his way to the microphone. The Treasurer apologized for the absence of committee members, Stephen and Jeff, called away on business. He then introduced Arun as the GP for the Village and, maybe soon, for the nearby small town. There was loud clapping for Arun.

When things quietened down, Arun said, "Ladies and gentlemen, I chose to come to this Village from London when the NHS HQ told me the town had had no GP for 2-3 years. I volunteered to come here. As many of you may know, I also practice ophthalmology in the hospital, performing operations, on Wednesday afternoons, Saturdays, and Sundays. I owe my gratitude to the Howard family for the smooth functioning of the Surgery and the clinics to my wife, Elizabeth Howard. We were married in the Registrar's Office in the next Town. She is now my PA for my private practice.

When I came here, I saw the Village had people but no life. Due to a lack of job opportunities, young people are leaving for other towns. I can offer employment to a few people. But it does not end with that.

I wanted to make this Village my hometown where Elizabeth and I can bring up our children like all others and grow old with dignity. I want the same benefits for all of you. We are equal partners striving for the growth and wealth of the Village.

Towards this, I have suggested some initiatives this weekend. For organizing this part of the project work, I thank Liz and Chris for their help and all the volunteers who collected and processed the questionnaires distributed. Also listed are facilities to be provided by the Council. Arun indicated the boards and continued, "It is apparent that the Village community wants better facilities for their children, as the next generation should be better off than them. Not a bad idea to aspire. One could wait for the local councils to help, but that could take a lot of time. You all want bread today, not jam tomorrow. I am here to see how, with your help, we can go about it."

Mr. Fisher spoke, saying, "On behalf of the Village Committee I would like to say how pleased we are to have such a large crowd – the highest ever – for this year's bank holiday event. Credit should go to Dr. Ayer and his team for wanting to develop the community. We, as the village committee, will do all we can to help Dr. Ayer and his team and provide assistance in seeking council funding and free lease of property for the use of the children of tomorrow. We eagerly await tomorrow's update."

There were no question and answer sessions planned at this early stage.

That evening, the post-dinner discussion centered around the days' events and the positive responses received from the residents. They all felt that it was a good start, and more benefits would result in making the Village a growing and thriving community with Arun as a catalyst.

The next day saw a huge crowd visiting the grounds, and the stalls raked in a lot of money. The weather was sunny, and the demand for food and souvenirs exceeded all expectations. The village community was happy and moved around with an extra spring in their steps. They were eager to listen to Dr. Ayer and find out what he had planned for the village and small-town communities' revival. Liz and Chris had feedback from the volunteers on the skill levels required for primary school, training, and other areas. Jessica and Chris had inputs from people interested in surgery work in the areas of midwifery and nursing, respectively, and they had shortlisted candidates for further consideration.

At 2:30 PM, Arun took the platform after the summary of the day's events by the Treasurer, Mr. Fisher.

Arun began by saying, "I would like to convey my gratitude and that of my team's, on the robust response to our questionnaires, not only from the Village but also from the small Town. The feedback since our last meeting has been excellent.

The community overwhelmingly supports the need for a kindergarten, protected play area for toddlers and young children, grounds for playing football, cricket, hockey and tennis, and the need for additional centers for developing social and career skills.

Responses also show that there are people with teaching experience willing to look after kindergarten. The Village Committee has agreed to provide a small area as a protected playground; inquiries are afoot regarding obtaining a substantial ground for young adults to play team sports. The estate agent has offered an old barn previously used as a stable, at a nominal price. The Village Committee is considering the purchase of this warehouse with local council funding. There are willing masters/tutors, both men, and women prepared to train the youngsters in a few areas like auto mechanics, carpentry, electrical work, etc. I also asked teachers to help students with physics, chemistry, mathematics, and other subjects to assist school-leavers with their preparation for university entrances. I am waiting for those responses.

Gazing into my crystal ball, it looks like we can start in the areas mentioned today. It would take between one and three months to provide park facilities. It may take longer to finalize the purchase of the warehouse and obtain equipment for skills training, for which we will be seeking corporate sponsors.

I look forward to meeting you all at the same time tomorrow for updates on various issues. If you have any queries, please let the volunteers know, so that I can respond to those tomorrow. We need the support of both the communities, and with the cooperative effort, we can encourage this small area on the UK map to grow and prosper. Thank you for the patient hearing."

Mr. Fisher thanked Arun and said that the meeting had opened their eyes to the community's latent talent and hoped Dr. Ayer with his team could channel his for the good of the next generation.

There was a standing ovation for Dr. Ayer and his team, including the volunteers, and the crowd drifted out to the tea stalls.

Arun and the rest of the family, along with Debra and Sandra returned to the house for coffee and further evaluation of candidates and events.

Barbara said regarding the event, "I have never seen anything like it before in all the 30 years I have lived here."

They had dinner, and after that, they generally spoke about politics, sports, and fashion. Arun, went to his office, newly converted by Barbara, to study the various CVs and made notes on each candidate for the upcoming interviews.

Monday was also an enjoyable, sunny day. The volunteers gave more forms to various people in the Surgery and updated the shortlists already made. They then gave them to Arun.

The representative from NHS HQ came at noon. The Village Committee welcomed him. Arun met them towards the end. The representative said he had come to observe, listen, and go back with the residents' feedback on the GP surgeries. The representative also said that he had no other plan and would like to meet the Village Surgery staff. Arun introduced all of them, and the people who had helped him settle in quickly like Dave and Sally, Dick, the Bank Manager, and the Registrar, who conducted his marriage with Liz. Then the committee took the NHS representative for snacks at the stalls. The representative was impressed with the marquee, booths, and all arrangements. He was amazed to see such a large crowd for such an occasion. He said even in London he had not seen such groups for a bank holiday weekend event. He realized that the people were there because they wanted to hear Dr. Ayer and his plans for the Village and Town and how they could benefit. Mr. Fisher briefed him about the ideas, and he was impressed. After that, he thanked the committee and left by 2:00 PM.

At 2:30 PM, people gathered for the final session of plans for the area.

Arun said, "We have had overwhelming support from the residents in the whole area, covering the village and the small town. We have made some progress in our discussions. I'm happy to announce that the kindergarten school will be open for admissions ten days from today, operating in the community center. Work on converting the protected area into a children's park will start by Tuesday and should be complete in two weeks.

For the sports grounds, we are still waiting to get land allocated, and, hopefully, in 3-4 months, we will have more clarity. Indoor cricket will be in a used warehouse. The coaching for career skills will start three weeks from now. There are also tutors available for all school subjects for 'O' and 'A' levels. Those who want coaching should put their names on the board in the community hall.

All these are a welcome start to change the landscape of the area for the better. I hope I can count on your support and assistance as these projects take shape. I am sure when you all see changes for the better; then your support will automatically follow."

Everyone felt that it had been a wonderful weekend with many good things to happen. They were happy about contributing to the projects.

That evening after dinner, they all sat in the lounge.

Liz said, "Arun, you said that you were going entrust the task of finding sponsors to someone else. Who did you have in mind? I could do that until you find the right person."

Arun smiled ruefully, "I intentionally did not want to involve you in that responsibility, Liz. It involves a short trip. I did not want to miss you even for a minute."

"What? Are you jealous?"

"Very, and I am not ashamed to admit it. One of the issues with beautiful women is they attract attention from the opposite sex. It is also not about trust between husband and wife. It is the way of the world. I have other important plans where you will have a higher profile with the media in the future. You are going to be the 'Chief' for all the projects in those areas."

"Okay, sweetheart, I trust you. I promise never to go out of your sight!"

Chris sighed, "I thought you would have a surprise visitor for me. Not my lucky weekend, was it?"

Arun responded, "The visitor will be here next Friday by mid-day. He will be staying in our old apartment over the Surgery. As Liz and I will be at the hospital, I request you, Chris, to show him around. If he is willing, he will be our new Practice Manager."

"Hmm...have, you deliberately asked him to come when you are the hospital to set him up with me, Arun?"

Arun countered, "I could ask him to hang out at a seaside resort till Liz and I are free. Would you like me to do that, Chris?"

"It's not my decision. Though, if I find the Manager sort of stuck up, then he will be banished to the seaside resort."

Arun shrugged. They all expected Chris to jump at the opportunity, but when the situation arose, she had cold feet. Jessica said that Chris should do whatever she felt best, and she had her full support.

When Liz and Arun were in bed, Liz said, "It was a wonderful weekend. All enjoyed the Promised Land approach to the area. A lot of brownie points for you so far!"

"These are good signs, but the flip side is that now all their expectations are sky-high. If any of the projects falter or get delayed, their tolerance level will be deplorably low, and regard me as a failure. That is why I chose only modest projects to start with."

"Well, let's hope all goes well. You've certainly earned a bonus performance from me!"

CHAPTER 23

Reinforcements

Arun had a short meeting in the Surgery at 5:00 PM with all the potential candidates. He introduced Dave and Sally and explained their roles in the Surgery work. Arun stressed that the Town Surgery would start accepting patients from the following Monday, and one of the new receptionists would have to start taking appointments from Monday morning. Sandra would be there to help on the first two days. The other new receptionist would be in the Village Surgery, helping Debra for the early two days. Jessica would be in the Town Surgery two days a week – Tuesdays and Thursdays – so would Chris. Thus, a schedule was put in place to alternate the experienced staff with the recruits, so that both practices would run smoothly.

Arun also stated that there would be a Mr. Robert Smith coming in on Friday afternoon who would be staying in the apartment, which Liz had used for a short time. If selected, Robert would be operating as the Practice Manager for both the Surgeries and would release Arun from those management responsibilities. Once he settled down, the final decision of who worked where would rest with him.

As Liz was not involved in the NHS practices, she would not have to come to the Town Surgery. However, in the mornings, Arun worked in the Town Surgery he would return to the Village Surgery to have lunch with Liz and the other staff. Having lunch and dinner with Liz was a must for him.

They all were made aware of his abundant love for his wife, and they respected that. Many wives were jealous of the depth of love and affection showed by Arun to Liz, who blushed a lot at their gazes but inwardly enjoyed every bit of it.

They all left the Surgery and went to their respective homes. That evening

Chris said, "Arun, I am glad you selected the candidates, and they were all pleased with their jobs, salaries, and training. But you realize that this puts a lot of pressure on us – my grandma, Sandra, Debra, and me. When will we have the time to train them, besides doing our usual duties?"

Arun said, "We all have to extend ourselves during this early stage of taking the new staff with us. I request you to take some time for the new candidates before working hours or over the weekend to train for their roles in the Surgery work."

Jessica added, "You are right. We all have to put in the extra effort to train them and not talk about pressure at this stage. 'Shoulder to the wheel' is the motto for us all, and we should get on with it from tomorrow."

"And while you're making the schedule Chris, don't forget your commitment with Robert."

Chris laughed, "I completely forgot about babysitting the Practice Manager! I will follow your instructions, sir!"

They all laughed at Chris's comments and knew she was secretly looking forward to meeting Robert.

They had their dinner by 7:00 PM and were in the lounge having their coffee when the doorbell rang. Barbara was surprised to see the Village Committee headed by Mr. Fisher at the door. They came into the room. Barbara ordered extra coffee and tea for the nine unannounced visitors.

"We are sorry for barging in like this. We thought you would all be at home and did not want to come during surgery hours."

Barbara asked, "What is the urgency, and how may I help you all?"

"With Stephen leaving suddenly for business reasons and not expected to be back soon, we had a meeting, and I was selected as the Head of the Village Committee and also the Treasurer. We are one member short. We thought of asking Dr. Ayer but felt he would be extremely busy with managing two practices. We were all of the unanimous opinions that you, Barbara, should be the replacement for Stephen. Will you please accept our nomination?"

Barbara complained, "I have not dealt with any of the issues, except for a few, due to Arun's involvement."

Mr. Fisher said, "Most of the activities will be on the projects initiated by Arun and his team, so you are the right candidate for it."

Barbara looked around at the others for support, but they all seemed to agree with Mr. Fisher.

Barbara said, "Well, if you put me on the spot like this, I can hardly refuse. I hope that in the future, you may get a more willing candidate."

"That is for tomorrow. For today, you make the quota required by the committee. This unsolicited visit was well worth it."

They all left, and Barbara was speechless at what she had committed herself.

Arun said, "I'm sure you will do an excellent job, and you will be fair and consult more women in the Village than what any other committee member has done so far. It would be a good idea to have a sub-committee discuss issues with, besides the main committee. That will reduce your stress."

"That is a splendid suggestion! I will talk to a few women about being on the sub-committee."

Arun said, "you should ensure they are independent and not in any way associated with the maim committee. In that way you are not required to get any one's permission to do things"

Once in their bedroom, Liz smiled, "Mum has become a great admirer of yours. She respects you more than Chris or me. You are stealing our place under our noses – did you realize that, Arun?"

The next day, Arun interviewed the candidates for tutoring school-leavers and Mr. Fisher and Barbara. They all seemed to have more than the required credentials.

Arun remarked, "I am quite amazed that you all have such talent, and no one was aware of it so far."

Barbara replied, "They are very modest, unlike men in the Village. They are like gold mines. One has to dig very deep to get gold in gold mines; in these women's cases, their skills come to the fore only when the opportunity to reveal them arises. They will not brag about their skills – it's is not their way of doing things."

The candidates will tutor voluntarily for a year with a review at the end of it.

Mr. Fisher announced that a couple of rooms in the community hall would be available for the coaching classes until the warehouse is ready.

Barbara then said, "I request the five candidates to stay on as I have something important to say and need their help. I plan to have a sub-committee comprising of women for the village projects, and I want to know if any of you are willing to help me?"

They all agreed to join and expressed their thanks for being considered. The meeting ended, and they all left for their afternoon surgery duties while the candidates returned to their homes.

That evening, at dinner, Chris said, "Mum, last night, you were very concerned about being on the village committee, but now you are the Head of a sub-committee on your terms. Brilliant! We never thought you had it in YOU."

Jessica added, "Brilliantly handled Barbara. From now on, women will have a larger voice in the village activities and projects, which we have never enjoyed."

Barbara blushed, "Thanks, mum, and everyone else, for the compliments and support."

The next day was busy. Arun and Liz went to the hospital for his clinic. The security staff assured Liz that she should lock her door, and they would be walking past her office in case of more evil men masquerading as doctors or consultants!

Friday came around. Arun noticed that Chris's mind was elsewhere as she made a couple of quick diagnoses when an extended inquiry into the patient's history would have been better. They had complained to him about being fobbed off without being listened to thoroughly. It was the first complaint he had had since starting the Surgery, and he was not happy about it. He had Jessica with him when the two ladies made the complaint. He asked Jessica to sound out Chris quietly and tell her to pull up her socks and not worry about Robert. Jessica understood the implications and was cross with Chris.

She went to her room and told Chris about the complaints. It had been a blemish-free Surgery for the last two months till today. Her voice was harsh, and Chris was embarrassed for three reasons; firstly, for making such an error, secondly, that the patients had actually complained, and finally, both Arun and Grandma suspecting that her mind was preoccupied with the arrival of Robert. It pained her considerably, and she wanted to go home and cry. But she was grown up, responsible, and was expected to act her age. She got the names of the two ladies, who complained, and during her lunch break, she made two home visits, apologized for her error and listened to them at length, and then assured them that the diagnosis had not changed, but she had been wrong to rush hem. The ladies had known Chris since she was a toddler and were sorry that they had overreacted. They thanked her for making home visits to clarify the issue.

At lunch, they missed Chris. Liz said perhaps she had had to make some home visits. Sandra said that there had been no requests for home visits. Jessica and Arun glanced at each other and knew that she must have gone to see the two ladies who complained. They did not say anything. Liz knew because Chris had told her before she had left. Chris came in about 20 minutes into lunch and apologized for being late. She saw Arun, and he did not say anything. She thought he might be angry or disappointed with her, but he had his characteristic smile.

While she was having lunch, the two ladies walked in and went straight to Arun. They said they were impressed with Chris's home visits and dealing with all issues. They said their comments were not complaints. Arun said he was happy to hear their feedback and asked Sandra to record them as comments and no complaints so that the Surgery continued to have a clean sheet.

After they left, Chris said, "Doctor, I'm sorry I rushed them and made them feel uncomfortable. It won't happen again."

Arun said, "Chris, I am in a way glad it happened. Errors are a wake-up call to us not to become complacent. We should learn from minor mistakes and become cautious than significant lapses that may lead to critical consequences.

I know you must have aged in the last hour or so until you dealt with the matter, and I'm sure you also learned a valuable lesson in the process. You took measures to remedy it without being prompted – I appreciate that."

"Many thanks, Doctor, for letting me off the hook. Rest assured that the message has sunk in quite well."

They had finished lunch and were having coffee when Sally announced the arrival of a visitor. It was Mr. Robert Smith. He was 6 feet 2 inches tall, blond with brown eyes, and a boyish face with a twinkle in his eyes. Barbara was impressed and hoped Chris would like him too. Chris looked Robert over but started enjoying her coffee. Arun shook Robert's hands and asked him to join them for lunch. Sally brought out a plate of steaming pasta. He had a long car journey from London and declared that he was famished. Robert dived into his plate, and only after eating more than half his meal started noticing people. He apologized for his bad manners claiming that as he had not had any breakfast that morning. Robert was almost fainting on entering the Surgery. Once he had finished his meal, he had coffee. In the meantime, Dave took his cases upstairs.

Sandra knowing the significance of the afternoon, had canceled the few appointments Chris had for the clinic and evening surgery.

Arun said, "Robert, I have to go to the hospital. Liz and Chris will show you to your apartment, and then Chris will show you around. Please join us for dinner this evening. I will see you them."

Barbara introduced them all and repeated the invitation for dinner.

Robert asked, "Are you sure? You do not have to take unnecessary trouble as I can rustle up something simple for myself in the kitchen?"

"No problem at all, and you can come along with us when we go home after the surgery."

Then Liz and Chris took Robert to the apartment, where Liz showed him the facilities there. Liz then excused herself as she had some urgent tasks to attend. She mentioned that she and Dr. Ayer had been married a few days ago in the local Registry Office. Robert congratulated her and told her it was news to him. To the total reluctance of Chris, Liz left, leaving the two alone.

CHAPTER 24

Romance in the air

After Liz left, Robert turned to Chris, "Miss Howard or should I be calling you, Mrs so and so? I do not want to make any mistake by assumption, as I did with your sister."

"Oh, I am not married yet. You can call me Chris as we are going to work together."

"Thank you, Chris, and please call me as Robert from now on. I still have to get the final approval from the Doctor regarding my appointment."

Chris shrugged, " "What would you like to do now? Unpack, or freshen up and meet me in the kitchen for a cup of coffee."

"Clothes can wait. I will freshen up and come down in a tick."

Chris left the apartment and went to the kitchen. She was not able to make up her mind about Robert. He seemed quite pleasant and friendly, but cautious in that he did not want to make any mistakes and offend anyone. Maybe he would sus it out for himself in a few days and then behave generally without any inhibitions.

Robert went to freshen up quickly. He had found Chris quite attractive. She was tall and slender with angular features like her mum and Liz. She was not quite the beauty Liz was; however, Chris had a naughty look with a lot of twinkle in her very expressive eyes. Her words were measured, and she seemed very empathetic. He thought, might be due to the nature of her job.

Robert went to the kitchen and found Chris and Sally. They took their coffee and biscuits and drifted to the dining area.

Robert said. "Chris, please tell me about the staff in the Surgery, and who does what?"

"I will start from doctor onwards, the positions and duties of Liz, myself, mum, Gran, Jessica, Debra and Sandra, Dave and Sally. There is another Surgery in the small town that will be functional from the following Monday. So, there will be two surgeries on two premises, and initially, people will be working in both places, on a rotation basis. I will take you through all of this. As Practice Manager, you will be managing both these Surgeries."

Robert said, "Let me tell you, I was pleasantly surprised about the role of Practice Manager."

Chris flashed him a glance. "I am sorry if I've jumped the gun, and please ignore my comments as this role is at the sole discretion of the doctor to decide."

"I assure you that the doctor did talk about the possibility of that position if the interview on Monday was successful and I merited the appointment here."

Chris smiled, "I am relieved that I did not say anything out of place. Since the Surgery will be closing at 5:00 PM, I suggest you sort out the room and your cases now, so that you can come with us in the car to the house. Usually, our Friday evening discussions run on till midnight, and it may be wise to be involved in this family practice, and in one evening, you will get to know more about all of us. You are welcome to stay with us overnight."

"I will do as you suggest. The more information I have before Monday's interview, the better for me. If I do not fit in here, I will know by the end of the night. I might not fit into the intimate group of your family, as I have hitherto been a loner. I must warn you that I'm good in small doses only."

Robert left to unpack and came down around 4.50 PM with an overnight case. He requested Chris not to tell anyone that he had come prepared to stay the night stay as he wanted to play it by ear.

At dinner, the visitor was the main attraction, and everyone warmed to him. Robert was very amiable with all the staff and had no airs. The maid brought cold drinks, and they went into the garden. Jessica, Chris, and Liz drifted to the conservatory on the pretext of seeing some plants, and once inside, they closed the doors. Barbara noticed it but did not comment. Arun and Robert were deep in discussion about the Surgery.

Liz turned to Chris at once, "Tell us all about what you said and did with Robert? Have you elevated him to heartthrob status yet?"

Jessica laughed, "Liz, let her slowly study him. There is no need to commit herself one way or another now itself."

"Liz, the omens are neither good nor bad so far. He is very reserved, and he told me that he was 'good in small doses only' and that he has been a loner so far. His staying on here as a Practice Manager also depends on the interview on Monday. If rejected, he will return to London – so let's not jump the gun."

Jessica said, "Oh, that's just Arun's cautious way of not promising the earth at the start. He did the same to you both. So, let us be hopeful and wish him luck."

Liz pushed on. "Anything else worth knowing from your other interactions?"

"Well, he didn't know that you were married. After you told him, he asked me whether I too was married or still Miss Howard, as he did not want to be presumptuous, I told him I was still 'Miss' and asked him to call me as Chris as we would-be colleagues. He asked me to call him Robert and said that he was not sure about getting the job. It looks like he is one of those who would like to have issues clarified and would not take anything for granted. Maybe, it all has to see it in print!"

Liz giggled, "If he stays here and you both fall in love, will he expect you to write a memo to inform him?"

Jessica laughed, "Liz, why do you annoy your sister? Let things take their course. Are you taking him around over the weekend?"

Chris shrugged. "We have not discussed it yet."

They returned to join the others.

Arun announced that he had had an in-depth discussion with Robert and that he was delighted about the position of Practice Manager. Also, that as he and Liz were working in the hospital on Saturday and Sunday, Arun had assured him that Chris would show him around the area.

Barbara said, "You seem to have sorted out a lot within 30 minutes. Let us go to dinner and talk about other things."

Dinner was quite simple. It turned out that Robert was also a vegetarian, so he shared the same dishes for Arun and Liz.

Chris asked, "Robert, when did you become a vegetarian?"

"I have been a vegetarian since childhood. We have a large farm with cows, sheep, pigs, chickens, etc., which we raised and sold. We knew they were going to become meat. We all had such an attachment to the animals. Each had a unique name – to me, it was like killing a member of the family. Every time I ate meat, I wondered if it was one of our animals – which distressed me so much that I turned vegetarian."

Jessica said, "Robert, you have made me think about my continuing as a meat-eater. From tomorrow I too will try being a vegetarian."

Chris quizzed, "So did your entire family give up commercial farming and turn vegetarian? Do you have a problem if others eat meat?"

"Not at all. It is my personal choice. I have grown up amongst meat-eaters. I don't mind others eating meat as you are all doing today, but I choose not to have it on my plate ever."

Chris persisted, "How come you changed your line of work from farming? Do you have brothers and sisters who live with your parents?"

"I have two elder brothers, and they are married. They all help my parents. The income from the farm is not enough for all of us to live on, so with their blessing, I had a university education and sought work outside. Because of the low opinion city folks have about farmers, I too faced prejudice. Other children used to call me – filthy, smelly, uncouth, etc. Of course, what I experienced is much less harsh than anything a person of color or a nigger has to face. I empathize with them."

Chris raised an eyebrow, "How will you relate to us? We are on the opposite side of the spectrum from farm boys?"

Robert said, "People come in all shapes, sizes, thoughts, and actions. One has to deal with it all. You are all nice people, but we all have to go back to our comfortable corners and view the world. I have no intention of enforcing my views, and it is not my remit. If I had to emulate your values to be one of you, then that will never happen. I am happy with where I am with my thoughts and actions. My expectations are set at a modest level so that I do not have to suffer much from disappointment. So, Chris, I respect your side of the spectrum as much as I am proud of my side of the spectrum."

Arun intervened, "To be fair, we are all in the same spectrum of trying to make an honest living and helping the community in the process. For that, we are all on the same side. Our views are convergent towards that ideal. The two ends have found common ground. People might have been on opposite sides at one time but are no longer, at present."

Barbara smiled, "Nicely said Arun."

Arun: "I like to say something about myself that I have not told anyone but Liz. Liz is from a very renowned and affluent family, and I'm at the absolute opposite end of the spectrum. I was an orphan – my mother left me a few hours after my birth outside an orphanage in Madras, a city in India. I never found out who my parents were. I qualified as a medical doctor and practiced in India. When I had sufficient training, I moved to the UK. I am a confident man who has only my merit as a recommendation. Despite knowing my humble beginnings, Liz was willing to take me on. So, Robert never worry about what you were and where others are. If fate takes you to new pastures and to people who think you are worth following, hold on to them like a precious diamond, never to lose but cherish."

Barbara gasped, "I never knew you were an orphan. You have come a long way – from rags to riches – a wonderfully motivational story. Liz didn't mention a word to us."

Liz said, "Arun did ask me to think it over, discuss it with all of you. He even suggested I visit the orphanage in Madras before making up my mind about marriage. I would have none of it. I was madly in love with him, and what he is now is more important to me than his past. The decision I made to marry Arun is the best decision I have made in my life."

Chris said, "I did not know your background Arun, but it only boosts my admiration for you to have come this far, fighting all odds."

Robert said, "Doctor, I did not know about your past and am ashamed that I have been taking of my past as something unique. My hardships are nothing compared to yours. I have parents, and you had none; we had a farm, you had only the orphanage; we had some income and you had only utter poverty. Considering all this, I request you all to forget what I said before, and I sincerely apologize for taking a high moral ground."

Barbara said, "We never took it amiss. Let's go to the lounge for coffee."

They all retired to the lounge. Arun and Liz took their coffee and went to sort out Saturday's event. Barbara and Jessica drifted towards the garden with their coffee. Chris was alone with Robert.

Robert said, "Chris, I hope you were not too offended by my remarks that you will not show me around for the next two days."

Chris laughed, "You did piss me off with your righteous comments! But your explanation later softened the blow. Of course, I will show you around the small Town and the Village and tell you about the practice.

"I am delighted that the Doctor asked me to be the Practice Manager, which means that I will be in charge of all staff on administration matters, not clinical issues."

"Correct. Your jurisdiction over me, other nurses, and all other clinical staff will pertain to admin; that too, on an advisory basis only. We, the clinical staff, will directly report to the Doctor, as he is also the sole partner for the Surgery business."

"That's settled then. When should I be ready?"

"10:00 AM should be adequate. We will do the small Town on Saturday and to the Village on Sunday and leave Sunday evening free to prepare for a Monday start."

Robert said, "That is wonderful. I would like to go back now to the Surgery, but I need a key to enter and exit. I like to jog in the mornings."

Chris replied, "Perhaps you should spend the night here... Feel free to run on the grounds where – we have 50 acres of land, a lake, and so on. Thankfully, there are no dogs to chase you."

Robert excused himself as he had had a long day and went to his room.

Barbara said, "Chris, you asked very pointed questions, and he answered like he wanted to prove a point. What do you think?"

Jessica intervened and said, "It is better to see it in the right context.

He has come here for the first time. He was overwhelmed by seeing the property and the vastness of the grounds. Also, a style of life very different from theirs. Your phrase "other end of the spectrum" must have spurred him into being defensive."

"I wish I had rephrased that," Chris sighed. "His defensive reply indicates that he was hurt by what I said. I was annoyed more with myself for provoking him like that, than by what he replied. In the future, I should follow Arun's advice on using one's brain before opening the mouth."

Jessica said, "If he is not your type, then move on. Just treat him as a colleague. You are still young."

Barbara, too said, "As mum says, don't rush into anything. You have always used your head, and that will serve you well this time. Be careful, girl, before you commit to anything."

On that note, they dispersed. When Chris entered her room and was checking her briefcase and she found an unopened envelope. She opened it and saw it was an application from a school friend's mother, who used to be a nurse in the hospital many years ago. She had asked for a job as she had fallen on bad times. Her only daughter was married and in Australia, and recently her husband had a stroke and needed care.

Chris was very touched by the letter and went to Arun's room and knocked. Liz opened the door and asked her to come in as they were working on some details for the Village project. Chris showed the letter to Arun, and he, without any hesitation, asked Chris to contact her next day, give her a temporary loan of GBP 100 (which he handed over to her), and ask her to come for an interview on Monday. If her experience checked out, she could start as soon as she had arranged someone to care for her husband.

Chris was grateful to Arun for such quick decision and the sensitive way he had handled the issue by giving the lady the dignity she deserved in her hour of need. Much as she wanted to hug him, as he was married, her sister, she hugged Liz instead so that she could transfer that hug to Arun later. Smiling, Chris left their room and came to her place. She slept happily – her happiness stemmed from being able to help her friend's mum than from seeing Robert.

CHAPTER 25

Reality Strikes

The next morning, Chris's mind was in a perfect state of calm. There were no lingering thoughts about Robert. She was focused on seeing her friend's mum and looked forward to putting her mind at rest. Her feel-good factor was entirely due to Arun's generosity and to give GBP 100 as an advance, spoke volumes about Arun's thoughtfulness. She was glad that he was Liz's life partner and now part of the family.

She met Robert at 7:30 AM in the dining room. Arun and Liz had already left for the hospital. They would have their breakfast there as usual.

Robert looked downcast. "Bad news from home. My mum was admitted to hospital last night with chest pain. They said it was a mild heart attack, and she should take it easy for two months. She's just 50 years old and spent all her life working hard, waking up at 4:00 AM each morning to milk the cows."

"I am sorry to hear that, Robert. Were there any stress factors?"

"Dad has a loan of GBP 20000 on the farm paying 18% interest. The high interest is crippling us and preventing us from meeting the basic needs of the livestock, not to mention that of the family. They have not had a holiday in the last five years, and they feel the strain, including the four children, my nieces, and nephews."

Chris sighed, "That's tough luck. What are you going to do?"

Robert said, "I did manage to speak to the doctor and Liz before they left. I apprised him for the whole situation, and he was very sympathetic. Of course, I will have to return to the farm and help my family out at this critical time."

Chris asked, "What did the doctor advice?"

"He was marvelous and said he would pay GBP 20000 to clear the bank loan, and we need to pay him only 3% interest. He also advised me to go back, be with the family, and manage their affairs till they are out of the red. He wanted me to request the banks to send the papers to him to clear the outstanding loan."

Chris said gently, "I am happy that the doctor has offered a solution. We are sorry that you will not be working here, but for you, duty call and your family comes first."

Robert said, "I don't understand why he gave up 1/2 a million GBP income in the city for these comparatively lowly paid GP jobs. The NHS HQ requested him to come out here as a GP, taking advantage of his benevolent nature. He has made a sacrifice, but people here might not know or appreciate it."

Chris said, "Well, all I can say is that this area has become a better place after he took over as GP. Initially, people disliked him due to his color. They all have changed their minds and now eat out of his hand. What are your plans now?"

Robert said, "I want to make an early start. If you can drive me to the Surgery, I will drive off to see my mum and convey the good news regarding the loan. I am sure it will speed up her recovery. Please convey my thanks to your mother and Jessica for a wonderful dinner and hospitality."

"I will do so; let us leave now."

On reaching the Surgery, Robert packed in ten minutes and left at once to return to his farm. Chris felt sad but also relieved. The relationship she had developed in her mind would never have worked out. She had sensed it during their discussions the previous evening and Robert's 'high moral ground' comments.

She went to her friend Lisa's house, to see her mum and dad. They were at home and welcomed her, apologizing for the room's state as they had not expected to see her.

Chris saw that Lisa's father was able to move around inside the house with a walking stick and take care of his WC needs and shower. He needed help only for cooking and cleaning. It was quite comforting to note that he was not dependent on his wife.

Chris said, "The doctor read your letter and was very moved by it. He asked me to give you this advance and tell you that there is a job for you in the Surgery, full-time, from Monday onwards. He would also like to see your husband as a patient on Monday in Surgery and take over his medical care."

Katie (Lisa's mum) was profoundly affected. "The doctor's actions so much touches us, and are so moved. We thought there was no hope for us here and no friends. You are like a messenger of God!

I can work a full-time job as Stan can cope with most things. As the clinic is only ten minutes away, I can come home for lunch and check on him. I will be delighted to work with you and share my experiences. You are like a daughter to me, Chris, and we see Lisa in you.

I understand Liz married Dr. Ayer. I wish her all the best. We keep track of developments in the Village and how nicely the GP Surgery was. Everyone is in praise of Dr. Ayer and his team. We saw him in action on the bank holiday weekend event."

Stan said, "Please tell the doctor that I will see him on Monday. He has brought a lot of relief to a suffering family by offering a job to Katie. We are ever so grateful to him and you, Chris."

Chris hugged both of them, tears in her eyes, and left.

She returned from her Mission of Mercy and briefed her mom and grandma on all the morning's developments.

Jessica sighed, "In a way, the worrying issue of whether Robert's suitability got resolved. So, you can start again with a clean slate now."

Barbara said, "Well, I guess that's that. Marjorie has invited us all for a ball in her house next Saturday as her daughter is getting engaged. I told her that I would let her know in a day or two. I was not sure whether Arun would come or not."

Chris said, "Mum, never even contemplate Arun forgoing his clinics.

He can miss the Surgery work but never the ophthalmology clinics in the hospital. I am not sure whether Liz will come without him. He usually has stressful clinics with the operations, and he needs her all the time. We three could go."

"I agree with Chris. Let the three of us go. Confirm it with Marjorie this evening," Jessica suggested,

Barbara agreed to do so,

When Liz and Arun were driving to the hospital, Liz asked, "Arun, you decided very quickly about giving Robert a low-interest loan. What made you do that?"

"Firstly, from the way he spoke to Chris, I could tell his heart was not in the right place. Secondly, they paid a hefty interest rate of 18% on GBP 20000, which in itself is about GBP 3600 per year. They were struggling; I thought by giving them a low-interest loan of 3% they would save about GBP 3000 per year; finally after he took the high moral high ground for a simple question of hers. I felt it would be difficult for Chris to spend a lifetime with such a person. It was better he left the area. That's why I gave him the loan and advised him to work on the farm. I am glad he took it."

Liz smiled, "I am touched to note how much you feel for each of us and, in this case, acted quickly to save Chris from an attachment that will cause her misery."

"What are we, if we cannot sense the problems ahead and avert those well in advance. I am sure Chris will find a beau soon."

That evening they gathered to discuss the day's events and reminisce about the changes the last 48 hours had brought into their lives. The conversations were mostly on general issues, and peace prevailed in the house.

Barbara brought up the topic of Marjorie's ball.

Liz said firmly, "Both Arun and I are delighted that you have omitted us as there is a special meeting at the hospital on that day. We may even stay on in the hospital for the night."

Then Arun had a phone call from Robert. His family was delighted about the reduced repayments. Robert's mum, too, was recovering well and sent her thanks and blessings.

Sunday was a quiet day, and Chris was busy going over some study material. She had been reading them, making notes for the last four weeks, and had another eight weeks of training to go. If Chris passed the test, then the RCN board would elevate her to the level of Senior Nurse, an achievement to get qualified at such an early age. She was hoping that with the two surgeries, Arun may make her a 1/3 partner in the Surgery. She, therefore, decided to put her heart into hours of reading and learning procedures.

As she was lying on the bed, her thoughts circled Arun. She was grateful for his careful planning and extreme sensitivity to issues affecting all of them. But for his intervention, she may have drifted into a going-nowhere relationship with Robert.

Her mind wondered about other suitors. She had not found anyone so far, not that she was looking. Only Liz's whirlwind marriage had brought her suppressed emotions to the surface, and she too wanted to have an excellent life partner. She knew she was still young at 26 and need not rush into a wrong decision. She was not keen on working anywhere other than this area (the Village and small Town). Her chosen partner should be willing to stay here with her, in this house, without his ego being affected. She had a lot of friends in the area during school days, but hardly any remained. Perhaps, Arun might fix her up with someone else soon. Little did she know that fate was going to take a hand in her life.

CHAPTER 26

Gala night and Fate intervention

Sunday was a busy day for all of them. Chris met the nurses to find out how they were preparing for the next day. Then she came to the Village to see Lisa's mum, Katie, who showed her the new dresses she had bought to wear under the white coat during surgery hours. Lisa's dad was exceptionally perky, and there was a spring in his step due to life looking up at last. Chris and Katie encouraged him to walk outside and took him to the community hall. Once inside, after negotiating the five wide steps without their assistance, he entered the room and was very happy to read all the notices and read the papers and magazines.

They happened to bump into Mr. Fisher there. He was delighted to see his old friend, Stan, out and about, and Stan told him how happy he was to get out at last. Inspired, Chris asked Mr. Fisher whether it would be possible to have a couple of rooms in the hall during weekends only. There were at least six people in the Village affected by a stroke, and she was sure a similar number, if not more, would be found in the Town as well. She wanted to use the weekends usefully, like Arun did, to help those affected people by bringing them here as part of their physio treatment. Seeing them would also improve the morale of other people and benefit the community. He agreed and showed her two rooms, which she could use. He also suggested a separate place for the stroke victims to sit and read in and move around without interruption.

Chris came home and told her mum and gran about her morning visits and discussion with Mr. Fisher. Barbara was pleased with Chris's public-spiritedness and left for a meeting in the community hall. Jessica decided to stay and walk around the estate and enjoy the beauty of the lake. Chris joined her gran.

"Grandma, I am ashamed to admit it, but last night I almost hugged Arun, and I have to say had some naughty thoughts about him. Am I not terrible?"

Jessica squeezed her arm. "Chris, it's natural to feel that way. In my younger days, I was quite naughty and had kissed and cuddled many boys in school or the park without my parents' knowledge!"

"Did you? I am stunned by your revelations."

"But Chris, please dismiss any sexual fantasies you have about Arun, as these will complicate the peaceful family life we have finally achieved. An affair with Arun will split the family forever. My husband and your dad had several extra-marital relationships with native African women in Botswana. No one here ever came to know of it. But in this small Town, any such scandal will spread like wildfire. Be grateful to Arun for the wonderful opportunity he has given you. People here will soon look up to you with pride and wish their daughters would be equally responsible. Don't ruin it for a moment of passion. Act sensibly and responsibly. If you cannot control your feelings, then avoid being with him on your own. He will never do anything to hurt Liz, and he has no eyes for any other woman besides Liz. So never tempt him."

Chris said, "I will never stoop to seducing him, and I will never drag the good name of the family down. You can trust me, Grandma."

They walked around the small lake, which used to be full of moss and algae but now had clear water, they could see fish in the lake. Then they met Philip, one of the gardeners.

"Philip, what has happened to the lake? Now it has fish swimming around!"

"Madam, it was all due to the Doctor. He saw the lake full of moss and algae and told us to clear it. He paid each of the five men GBP 20 to do so. He asked us to put special salts to neutralize the water. When it had neutral pH after testing, we introduced some fish, which has now multiplied. There are even frogs, millions of them, now. We hope he does not tell us to introduce an adder to control the frog population!"

Jessica smiled, "Thank you, Philip. Continue with your good work. Our regards to your family."

Later, Jessica remarked to Chris that Arun's dynamism extended to everything, even beyond the medical. All the area's projects depended on his leadership, direction, and limitless enthusiasm.

Philip led them to the vegetable plot, which was different from what Jessica and Chris had known.

Philip said, "Again, the change is due to the doctor's suggestion. Being a vegetarian, he took a keen interest in developing this plot – short of doing the actual gardening himself."

Chris explained, "He has a good reason for avoiding gardening. He does very complex operations on the eye. Any cuts or bruises on his fingers might affect his ability and endanger the surgery outcome."

Jessica said, "I did not realize that. We must ensure that he is taken good care of by all of us."

In the evening dinner, Jessica narrated the events of the day and their conversation with Philip.

Liz said, "Arun, I didn't know you had taken such an interest in the grounds?"

Arun said modestly, "While jogging, I noticed these things and made a few suggestions to Philip. Sally helped with the vegetable plot, and they even put paving around the lake on my suggestion so that we can walk around safely during the rainy period. All credit goes to them."

Barbara changed the subject. "I had a productive meeting with the committee, and we discussed what facilities needed for the modification of the warehouse. They were also impressed with Chris's idea of group physio exercises for people recovering from strokes in the area."

Chris quickly filled in Arun on her scheme of combining exercise with an opportunity for stroke victims and their Carers to get out and socialize in a safe environment.

Arun said, "It is a splendid idea, and coming from a nurse, they will treat this as a logical step in healthcare for the suffering patients. I'll speak to someone tomorrow to offer you specialized physio training later this week."

Chris was grateful that he encouraged her initiative.

Modifications to the park for the children had already taken place. The delivery of some equipment like slides, swings, etc., were due by Tuesday. The park would be ready by Thursday, eight days ahead of schedule.

Notices were up in the community hall posting a tutoring schedule for students appearing for their 'O' and "A" levels. A few students had already enrolled. Liz had been busy scheduling the project work in these areas and helping with the orders of equipment and furniture, even though the committee members did the central part. Her mum ensured that the committee did most of the work and that Liz played a supervisory and more visible role. Barbara also involved her sub-committee at each stage and had valuable contributions from them on various issues.

Time passed, and the night of engagement invitation descended on them quickly. Chris, her mum and gran left at 5:00 PM for Marjorie's place. There was a sizeable gathering there, and Chris found a few of her old school friends. Three out of five girlfriends were already married and were there with their husbands. Two were single like her and waiting for suitable grooms. They were unemployed despite having excellent qualifications. Nicola had skills in science was excited to hear about voluntary work in tutoring students. As she was interested, Chris asked her to come to the community hall the next morning.

The four boys she studied with were all married and had come with their wives. After the initial formalities and handing over the gift, she circulated, drink in hand. She spotted a good-looking man standing quietly in one corner. Their eyes met, and he then strolled towards her. She also went forward to meet him. After the preliminaries, he told her his name was Harry White and that he was a Practice Manager in a GP practice. As he was the only son and heir, and his aging parents needed assistance, he had decided to come back to the small town.

Chris introduced herself and her mother and grandmother, who joined her. Jessica immediately said, "How good to see you! Aren't you, Harry? You were a young boy when we last met. How are your parents, Julie and Tom?"

Harry responded warmly, "Good to see you as well. My parents are fine. Thank you. How is your husband Stephen – did I get his name, right?"

Jessica smiled, "Yes, you did. Where are you staying now?"

"We are moving to the lane by the lake. Our house is one of the two houses with a compound wall. My parents bought it two months ago, and we are moving in tomorrow."

Barbara exclaimed, "How lovely! We will be neighbors. Tell us about yourself, Harry."

Harry smiled, "I was in South Africa for six years and then came to London for studies. Things were not good there in South Africa. A close friend asked me to help his friend, a GP in North London and looking for a Practice Manager. I enjoyed working for the GP for the last five years. However, due to my parents coming here and wanting to settle in the Village, I reluctantly had to resign my job in London. Here again, my friend suggested visiting him, and I intend to meet him on Monday."

Barbara said, "Well, my son-in-law, Dr. Ayer, is the GP here. I would like to invite you and your parents for dinner tomorrow so that we all can meet. Where are your parents?"

"Dr. Ayer is the GP I worked with earlier, and he is the one I'm meeting on Monday," beamed Harry.

Just then, an elderly couple came in and were warmly greeted by those who knew them from South Africa. The Sunday dinner arrangement was accepted. Barbara offered to send staff around to help with the unpacking and offered help in contacting any tradespeople whose services they may need.

Then the older group moved away to greet to see Marjorie and her daughter and

Chris and Harry were left alone.

Chris said, "My parents were in Botswana. My sister Liz and I used to visit them during the school holidays. We stayed with my grandma and did our schooling here. We went to the university here, where Liz specialized in Economics and Political Science. I took up nursing. Liz now works as a PA for her husband, Arun. I am the nurse in the Surgery in the village and supervise the nurses in the small Town Surgery. Arun is the GP for both the places."

"Liz is married. How about you?"

"No, I am single."

Chris then drifted away from him to join her mum and gran. After dinner, there was a dance and Harry wanted to have a dance with Chris. She declined, saying maybe next time. After the party ended, they returned home. Her gran and mum were thrilled to have such good neighbors.

Barbara asked, "Chris, what were you and Harry talking about?"

"He wanted to know about me, so I told him about being a nurse in the Surgery. He then asked me if I was married."

"Why didn't you dance with him?"

"Oh, I had too much on my mind to enjoy dancing. Harry seemed very nice. I wonder why Arun did not tell us about Harry coming here."

Barbara sighed, "Look, young girl, after the disappointment with Robert, he might not have wanted to raise our hopes in vain."

On reaching home, they all turned in. Chris was in her dream world. She could not but marvel at Arun's plans and how he managed to keep it a secret.

CHAPTER 27

Meeting of Minds

On Sunday, Chris went to meet Nicole in the community hall at 9:00 AM. She told Nicole that she could put her name down as a tutor for any subject Nicole chose and list when she would be free. She then went with Chris around the Village to see the park, the new protected play area for toddlers and under 3's, the surgery from outside, the Village shop, the café, the grocery shop, and other shops. They also went to Lisa's place to see her parents, and they were delighted to see Nicole after so many years. The three asked Stan to walk to the park, and slowly he managed to do that. Nicole left shortly after. Chris stayed with Lisa and Stan for a while. Lisa had called her last evening and thanked her tearfully for all the help she had rendered.

When Chris returned home, she saw the delivery van outside the neighbor's house and men moving around carrying furniture into the house. Her mum had sent some sandwiches, cakes, and tea for the new arrivals.

The afternoon went quickly in anticipation of the evening visit from Harry and his family. Liz and Arun finished work early. Arun had already briefed Liz about Harry on Saturday, and she was looking forward to meeting him.

The doorbell rang, and Barbara brought the visitors, and Harry was delighted to see Arun again. Arun and Harry withdrew to one corner of the room and spoke animatedly as long-lost friends. Harry's parents were delighted to see Arun as well. Harry did not get to talk to Chris before, during, or after dinner. They left as they had all had a long day – Harry telling Arun that he would be in the Surgery by 8:30 AM.

After they left, Jessica told Arun how she knew them in South Africa and had seen Harry as a young boy many years ago. Arun was surprised to hear of this previous connection between the families.

When Chris went to bed, her thoughts were full of Harry. He was good-looking, erudite, and well-spoken. He did not give himself airs and seemed to be a good listener. It could have come from being a Practice Manager in an extensive Surgery for some years. He seemed happy with his lot, not very ambitious or pretentious. She smiled at his question of whether she was married or not. "Is he interested in me?" she wondered. With a smile on her face, she went to sleep.

Monday was a busy day with Katie joining, and Harry coming to the Surgery.

Chris explained her tasks to Katie and asked her to shadow her for the first day. The patients warmed up to Chris more, with Katie by her side, as many knew her from childhood. They also felt that the new GP had brought the Village together by appointing familiar faces and giving employment to local people.

Back at her desk, Chris found a white envelope with her name and the word 'Confidential' written across it. Excited, she tore the letter open and read it eagerly. The messages contained two attached forms, which Chris signed, and at once with the urge to hug and kiss Arun. Then she mentally calmed down, thinking of what her gran had advised. A handwritten note inside said that Chris should see Arun at 2:00 PM and not discuss details with anyone until her meeting with Arun took place. She was restless, as she wanted to tell Liz, but Arun would come to know of it and would not share with her any more confidential information in the future. Chris reluctantly put the two forms in the envelope, wrote Dr. Ayer on the cover, and asked one of the trainee receptionists to give to him when he was free. She then put the letter in her folder and locked the cabinet.

During the morning tea break, Chris did not see Harry, and she thought, perhaps, he had gone back to his house to help his parents with the unpacking.

During the lunch break, Katie went to check on her husband, who had gone earlier on his own to the community hall, read the papers, and came back for his lunch.

Barbara said, "I have not seen Harry after he came. Has he gone back to his house, doctor?"

"I asked him to be the Practice Manager for the Town Surgery only, and that role will start next Monday. He has gone there to check out the location and facilities. Unless any of us goes to that Surgery, one is unlikely to see him here."

Jessica remarked, "We thought he would cover both surgeries."

Arun said, "I felt this Village surgery is going on well without a Practice Manager and asking him to take over here as well could ruffle feathers unnecessarily."

Barbara said, "That was a masterstroke – it's true; we may have resented his intervention."

Chris left the lunch group and went to see Arun at 2:00 PM to thank him for making her a partner for the two practices. The contract stated that she would earn 1/6 of the profits in the first year and 1/3 of the profits from the 2nd year onwards.

Chris, trusting Arun a hundred percent. She did not even bother to read the details. She had turned the page to look for the place where she had to sign and just put her name on both the copies. She had been on cloud nine the whole morning after signing the contracts. Katie had wanted to know what made her so happy, but she fobbed her off.

Chris thanked him profusely for making her a partner. "Even 10% of the profits would have made me happy as long as I am a partner. Much as I want to hug and kiss you, Grandma has advised me to control myself. I will stick to a simple 'Namaste' as per Indian tradition from now on."

Arun grinned, "I did not know you discussed your every urge with your grandma, but her advice is sound. If it's only 10% you want, then shall I change the contract?"

Chris said quickly, "No. 1/3 is just fine."

"Chis, you are entitled to a car, but please do not choose a fancy sports car. People should not perceive that we earn a lot and are living well when patient care should be the priority."

"Message understood. I assure you that I will be discreet about my salary rise and will not brag about it. I am truly grateful to you for making me a partner. Please tell me why you decided to do it now."

"I intended to do it from the very beginning, but it would appear as showing favoritism to a sister-in-law. So, I waited till you had a few nurses reporting to you. With Harry coming in, I do not want him to get the impression that he should also be a partner. Hence, I brought forward the appointment.

Ideally, I should have another GP as a partner as one GP cannot serve a population of 8000. One needs at least 3 GPs for that. For the moment, most residents are healthy due to simple food and physical work, which meant the surgery is less busy than average. We do not have a waiting list for appointments. But due to the aging population, this could change in 1-2 years. Until then, we can manage with one GP.

You can tell others about being a partner, but after the initial euphoria, please keep it under your hat. Keep a low profile and focus on the job of being a nurse in a rural practice. That secret of success is to understand, appreciate, and serve."

Chris did another 'Namaste' and said: "I will justify your confidence in me through my responsible behavior, and diligent execution of my duties and make you proud."

She went to manage her afternoon appointments. When she had about 20 minutes to spare, she phoned the dealership in the town, from where Liz had got her car and ordered a similar Austin Mini Estate in red (Liz's car was black). The salesmen said they had a car ready in the showroom and would deliver it within three days. Satisfied, she put the phone down and was walking on air until the next patient came.

At tea break at 3:30 PM, Chris went to Liz and told her about the partnership, which Arun had offered.

Liz congratulated her and said: "Arun mentioned it to me this morning while coming to work. He was concerned that delaying the offer could precipitate a problem with Harry and complicate things unnecessarily. I am so happy for you, sis."

"I am glad for whatever reason it happened. I have ordered a similar car to yours in red. Arun asked me not to buy an expensive car so that people think that NHS money is spent on perks."

That night, Chris told her mum and gran about the partnership and how happy she was. She also spoke about the new Austin Mini Estate that was going to be delivered on Wednesday.

Barbara said, "That is wonderful news, but it seems so sudden, doesn't it?"

Liz told about her conversation with Arun earlier in the day, and then they understood.

Jessica said, "Chris, he is taking good care of you. Behave yourself as I told you to."

"What did you tell her mum?"

Chris giggled and confided in her mum about her naughty thoughts about Arun and her grandma's warning her. "So, I told him from now I will stick to the traditional Indian custom of doing a 'Namaste' with both hands folded together. No more Western-type handshakes, hugging, or kissing. He will be forbidden territory for me from now on."

Jessica urged her once more to behave with dignity and pointed out that the best way to repay Arun would be by taking care of the Surgeries, giving him more time to focus on the clinics.

Liz said, "Arun will be setting up a separate clinic for ophthalmology to see the patients. The hospital also welcomed that because they have a long waiting list. Their facilities can be used only for operations and other complicated procedures. Arun also wants to do an evening every week to see poor patients for free."

Barbara said, "That's typical of him – always service-minded. Liz, you do not have to worry about any 'jerk' junior doctors making a pass at you."

Jessica suggested, "Why don't we convert my house for an in-patient stay?"

Liz said, "We are adapting the bungalow as a care home for the patients, who have to wait a day after the operation to ensure all is okay with them. Usually, it is a 1-2 day stay. The patients come with a relative or friend on the day of the operation, stay the night and leave the next day. In rare cases, the patient will be under observation for an additional day. Your house can take care of the overflow of patients from the bungalow."

"I will start working out a rental agreement tomorrow."

Chris said, "It all sounds wonderful, Liz. So, you have been busy sorting out all these issues."

Liz smiled, "Arun asked me to take the lead and make all the discussions. I will, of course, take his counsel before that. Gran, if it's alright with you, I will ask Dave to handle the modifications needed to make your house as a care home for at least four sets of patients. The bungalow annex will house the main theatre for the operations, and eight sets of patients can be accommodated there, besides my office."

Chris grinned, "Being a life partner, do you get 50%?"

"Correction -100%. And I usually give him GBP 2 each day for his expenses. I have been writing all the cheques since our marriage!"

Jessica sighed, "How wonderful! Your mum and I never enjoyed such privileges despite it being our money. We had to rely on our no-good husbands for cash that too, after grilling us!"

Chris said, "All has changed for the good, and you should make the most of it from now on."

They had dinner, but Arun had his dinner sent upstairs. They did not know what had cropped up suddenly so urgently. Liz knew he would tell her about it later. She did not want to tell the others that he had had some bad news about Harry from the NHS HQ in the afternoon.

CHAPTER 28

Neighbors Tragedy

That night Liz went up to her room early and saw Arun in bed. She asked him about what had happened.

Arun said he was very upset about Harry. It transpired that Harry had misappropriated funds from the Surgery he had been working in for the last four years, amounting to GBP 12000 – a considerable sum for any Surgery to cope. The single practice GP had trusted Harry to take care of the accounts, and somehow Harry had fobbed off the accountant at the end of each year.

Inland Revenue (IR), on routine auditing, had found extraordinary expenses allocated to cars, furniture, payment to temporary staff, etc., with no corroborating paperwork. They had questioned the GP who had passed on the query to Harry. Instead of responding, Harry had left suddenly.

The GP then called the accountant to the office, and the embezzlement had come to light. The accountant showed the queries he had raised over the last four years questioning Harry over those very expenses and warning him that IR auditors would scrutinize these. In the accountant's opinion, these were not legitimate Surgery expenses. The GP did not know about these exchanges, nor was he aware of these payments. The GP then sought NHS HQ help and showed them all the accountant's papers.

The IR audit department empathized with the GP but stated that he was ultimately responsible and fined. NHS HQ was sending an official with a warrant for Harry's arrest to the Surgery on Tuesday morning. They had taken Arun into confidence and asked him to summon Harry to his Surgery in the morning and allot a room for the official to interrogate him. Arun had agreed to that. He had already phoned Harry and summoned him for a meeting in his office at 9:00 AM on Tuesday.

Liz was shocked. "What a disappointment for all of us and, most importantly, for his parents!"

Arun said, "He was so amiable that even I believed him. Maybe the Surgery's laxness over the accounting gave him an opportunity. I will teach you accounts so that we can manage Surgery accounts together ourselves. There should be no room for mismanagement and loss of funds from the Surgery or any account."

Liz promised to keep an eagle eye on the accounts, so no misappropriation would ever occur.

Arun said, "By the way, your sister has a crush on me and has even told her grandma about it. Astonishing girl!"

Liz laughed, "She told the three of us she would only do 'Namaste' to you! I told her that you are out of bounds for everyone except me. For that, I expect a good reward now."

Arun smiled and obliged her.

The next morning, at 9:30 AM, the NHS HQ official arrived accompanied by two police officers. Arun asked whether a police presence was necessary at that early stage. Could they not hear his side of the story first before taking drastic action? They agreed and asked the police to wait elsewhere, from where they could come, if required.

In the meantime, Liz came to the office to pick up some papers, and Arun asked her to rearrange his appointments while he took the car and went to Harry's house.

He knocked on the door and saw Harry's parents, who wondered why he was there when he ought to be in his Surgery.

"Is Harry all right? Has anything happened to him?"

"Can I come? There is something I want to convey to you in utter privacy. It's bad news, I'm afraid."

Julie frowned, "Now you're making us nervous, Arun. The maid has gone to the market, and we have about an hour of privacy. Please tell us what the issue is,"

Arun sighed and brought them abreast of the situation. "The police will be speaking to you two. They requested me to see you and inform you. I can only forewarn you both that if you knew of any unexplained money movements in the last four years or, if you know if Harry has fallen into any debt, then it's up to you to reveal it to the IR. In similar cases, the officials usually take the person involved in London NHS HQ and then to prison, depending on the severity of the allegation and the unsatisfactory nature of defense put by the individual. They may send some officers to raid the house and take all bank papers and other documents they deem fit for their case. They will also get the bank to surrender all transaction details to them in confidence. I am sorry to be the bearer of such bad news, but I knew of it only now.

My advice to you is to seek legal counsel without delay. IR has a solid case supported by the accountant of the previous practice, who had queried Harry regarding the irregular expenditure. It appeared that the GP was left in the dark about those expenses, even though he is ultimately responsible for the loss of a considerable amount."

Julie looked flustered, "I hardly know what to say. We do not know anything about the money. We have enough money, and we have been sending him money rather than receiving from him. We are devastated and do not know what to do! Where is the NHS HQ? Can we pay the money back? Will that stop him from going to jail? Arun, we could sell this property to raise the money quickly. We bought it for GBP 30000 recently but will sell it quickly for 25000. Please advise us."

Arun said, "Please go to London and find a hotel close to the address I am going to give you. If he has been guilty of embezzlement, get your legal counsel to negotiate a settlement with the NHS. If you agree to pay the amount owed to the Surgery, then NHS and IR may overlook this as a crime and let him off with custodial service. It may be worth paying up. In any case, I urge you to engage competent legal counsel for Harry without further delay. If you have to sell the property, I will buy it at the price you bought it for and coordinate with the real estate agent, but we will get to that later."

Julie then talked to her husband and said: "Please give us the address of the NHS HQ. If you can help us with finding accommodation nearby, we will appreciate it."

Arun then phoned Liz, who told him that Harry, escorted by the two police officers, had been taken by car to London. Arun gave the phone to Julie, who had already surmised the bad news. The idea of her son taken to London under police escort was unbearable to both of them. They burst into tears.

After a few minutes, Julie regained her composure: "Arun, promise me that you will never subject your parents to such agony and disgrace in their old age."

Arun thought for a bit and then decided to come clean: "It will never happen in my case as I am an orphan."

Julie and her husband cried out loud and hugged him. "You have never known a mother's or a father's love in your life, yet you are a model son. God bless you and Liz and your family. May you all live happily!"

Arun asked her to pack a case for Harry along with theirs. Liz came to the house to help. She had already booked accommodation for them in London near the NHS HQ. On seeing Liz, Julie's tears were not controllable. But Liz enabled her to pack and gave her GBP 500 to tide over their expenses in London. Julie treated Liz like the daughter she never had. They dropped them off at the station to catch the London train. It was a sad finale to their dreams of living in the Village and enjoying country life.

On the way to the Surgery, Arun told her what Julie said and how distressed they were. They wanted to sell the house at less than market value to pay off the money owed to IR and the GP. They had handed over a key to the house just in case. They would never settle in the Village now. Sad, sad, very sad, he said to Liz.

At the lunch break, the staff surrounded Arun, wanting to know all about it. The news stunned all the team, most of all, Chris. She could not believe her ears and asked whether he thought that Harry was guilty. Arun said that he did not know, as he had not talked to Harry.

A somber mood prevailed for the rest of the lunch period. The afternoon session went by quickly, and Chris's mind was all about what she would talk about and hear about Harry from Liz and Arun.

In the evening, Arun gave them more details about the amount swindled during the four years and the accountant's report on expenses incurred. Jessica felt very sorry about the tragedy that had befallen her old friends.

Liz announced, "If Julie has to sell the house, then Arun thinks of buying it. We seem to be picking up property right, left, and center."

"I regard it as a Godsend for all the projects I have in mind. This property comes with large grounds – useful for our school and sports facilities. Slowly, slowly we will build up the infrastructure."

At dinner, the talk was mostly about what would have been, if Julie had been there. Julie did call to let Arun know that she had checked into the hotel and would visit the NHS HQ and let them know of any new developments. She was hoping to close the issue quickly with the payment of money and hoping that NHS HQ, would let Harry off with a slap on the wrist. Arun wished her the best of British luck.

There was a call from the NHS HQ official thanking him for liaising with Harry's parents. As they had promised to pay the full amount of GBP 11500 within a week, the GP had agreed to drop the charges. The GP would pay the tax overdue, with no penalty, and the issue would be closed. On the transfer of money, and NHS would release Harry, but blacklist him to prevent him from working in any other NHS practices or government service. The parents were already seeing their solicitor about raising the money. So, the official thanked Arun for his constructive intervention. It appeared that Harry had fallen in with a wrong crowd and had run up gambling debts. The carelessness of the GP he worked for had provided him with an opportunity to defraud. Arun was relieved and conveyed the news to the others. All were happy at the quick resolution.

Julie phoned again to say that she had taken Arun's advice regarding the financial settlement, and Arun could go ahead and contact her solicitor regarding the purchase of her house. She was enormously relieved that there was no prison prospect for Harry, and he appeared to have learnt his lesson. Arun wished them good luck once again and said goodnight to both of them.

CHAPTER 29

Projects Galore

The next day was quite busy. Julie phoned Arun in the morning to give details of her solicitor and bank account for the money transfer. Arun went to see his solicitor and got the paperwork organized for the house purchase and made money transfer on the same morning, which enabled Julie to get Harry released.

The Harry saga was over, and Arun's purchase of their property was underway, the family turned their attention on the projects. Chris found out the rooms in the community hall had a rotation put out for tutoring, and the children's playground was already complete with the installation of swings, slides, and other play equipment for children under five.

The warehouse was made suitable for playing games; and indoor cricket batting and bowling practice would be possible shortly. There was a separate section for badminton, basketball, and boxing. Now the young adults had somewhere to let out their steam and aggression. Tea, coffee, colas, chips, and sandwiches were also available.

The Village and the Town looked different from what they had done for the last 20-30 years. The Town Surgery was up and running. The staff has completed their training, and they were bright and eager. So healthy and active was the country people that there was no need for booking appointments. Most patients could walk-in. The system was ticking like clockwork, for which due credit to Chris and Liz.

The bungalow renovations were almost complete, and Arun had started seeing patients there on weekdays from 5:30-7:00 PM. The hospital management had inspected the facilities and was happy to send patients to the village.

The exams for 'O' and 'A' levels came too soon for the students and the tutors. The results still showed a definite improvement in the scores. The expectations were much higher for next year's exams. More young people had begun traveling there to avail of the free coaching, and the initiative soon attracted media attention. Liz was the spokesperson for the projects, and her beauty merited even more praise from the media. The journalists were so captivated by her that they interviewed her again and again. She enjoyed it, and she enjoyed teasing Arun about his jealousy even more. More importantly, the NHS HQ took notice and elevated Arun's status by conferring an award on him and invited him and Liz for talks in London.

Liz was the darling of the media. That was what Arun wanted for her – a high profile, proper use of her talents, a sense of achievement. He was slowly achieving that. Liz knew of his plans and was milking every ounce of it to her advantage. She had become a local celebrity. Many organizations invited her to address them, as they knew Arun was too busy.

Liz began avoiding traveling and instead invited media and organizations to interview her at the Village and see the progress. These also brought additional business to the local shops and hotels. Due to his work commitments, Arun refused to Chair many committees. Arun did all his hospital operations in the Village ophthalmology unit – which reduced the waiting list at the hospital and brought more income into the Village.

Chris had become busier, traveling between the two Surgeries and having physio sessions in the community hall. These also attracted attention from the media, and she needed to help neighboring counties set up similar units. NHS was impressed that at minimal cost and by involving local people and local facilities, Chris had created an innovative and positive rehabilitation process. This passion for community service captivated the media and impressed the NHS. At every stage, she never forgot to emphasize that the driving force behind all these changes was the arrival of Dr. Ayer – and his coming to the Village was heaven sent.

With all the media attention, the Village and small town grew in fame and attracted new businesses and tradespeople. But, along with prosperity comes crime and conmen that cause unrest in peaceful communities. Those developments, and a suitable husband for Chris – were yet to unfold.

CHAPTER 30

Orphanage

With both surgeries running smoothly and enough volunteers to manage the various projects, Arun told the family members one evening, that he had made arrangements for all five of them to visit India for two weeks. The itinerary was already planned – four days in Madras, three days in Calcutta, and three days in Delhi, with a visit to Agra to see the Taj Mahal.

Arun said, "I spoke to NHS HQ yesterday and said we would like to take a two-week break. They offered two GP's who could stay in the two flats above the Surgeries. The two GP's are a newly qualified, husband-wife team and are very community-spirited individuals. They are British from Warwickshire but studied in Cambridge and got their medical degrees six years ago. They are due to visit us next Wednesday for a few hours to introduce themselves."

Liz said, "Chris, can you manage the GP's introduction to staff in both practices and describe the various procedures?"

Chris rolled her eyes, "Trust my luck! Two bachelors come, and they are pushed out by fate. The third, who comes, is already married! I have to take care of them while you waltz off somewhere with your heartthrob!"

Jessica laughed, "Do not worry, Chris, a better one will turn up unexpectedly."

Barbara said, "I always wanted to visit India. Thank you, Arun, for planning it."

Arun said, "Liz will handle all the expenses for this trip. In Madras, we will be staying in the Orphanage. The standard of accommodation will not be what you are used to – it will be modest but spotlessly clean. We will leave in two weeks London to New Delhi; New Delhi to Calcutta; Calcutta to Madras: and then, Madras to London. All by British Airways (BA). Liz will liaise with the travel agent in London and give you all copies of the proposed itinerary."

Liz said, "Thrilled to do it, and please note, it is my treat!"

Arun continued, "The Orphanage has 50 children now aged 1-18. There is a kindergarten, primary, secondary school, and a college providing university education. There are a lot of workshops for students to get experience and specialize in any trade. Guru Shiva Iyer, the present Head, manages all the above facilities. The place is called an Ashram (which means sanctuary) and not an Orphanage. He is about 82 and is expecting to handover this year to younger people."

Chris commented, "Can we assume that you have played a key role in the Ashram growth?"

Arun smiled, "Mr. Shiva Iyer will give you a history of the Ashram and its progress. I left the Ashram to come to London about eight years ago. They all respect me and call me affectionately, "Anna" (which means elder brother). Liz, as you are my wife, they will call you, "Akka" (meaning elder sister). You will all be overwhelmed by the love and affection exuded by the younger boys and girls. Don't expect Western courtesies of not touching strangers, saying please and thank you very often, etc. They mean well, and they want to ensure you are all treated with great respect."

Liz exclaimed, "I already cannot wait to see the Ashram. Do we have to visit other places at this time? Let's spend a week in Madras and return. Next year we can take a longer vacation when we have two more GP's permanently in practice."

Barbara, too agreed, "The Ashram means more to us because of Arun. Let's cut the trip short to one week only as this is still a formative period for many of our projects here."

Chris and Jessica, too, murmured their assent.

Arun gave in, "Liz, can you please reorganize on that basis? At this stage, I agree that our focus on the projects here should be a priority."

The next morning Liz made the necessary bookings for travel through BA.

On Wednesday morning, at 11:00 AM, the new married GP's, Mike and Jenny, came. They had driven from London in a Ford Poplar. They seemed a very affectionate and well-matched couple.

Mike was 5 feet 11 inches, with brown hair and blue eyes. Jenny was a slim blonde, 5 feet 9 inches tall with blue eyes. Both seemed very reserved and shy.

Liz introduced herself and took them to her office, where Arun and Chris were waiting. After the preliminaries, Arun mentioned that Chris, who was his partner and younger sister to Liz, would take them over to the small-Town Surgery after meeting the staff and going over the processes in the Village Surgery.

At that moment, Barbara and Jessica entered the office, and Chris introduced them to Jenny and Mike. Arun and Liz then left for the ophthalmology center.

Liz told Arun while driving, "Arun, they seem like a nice couple and have three years' GP experience in a London surgery. Do you think they will agree to relocate here with reasonable incentives?"

"Liz, you beat me in thinking ahead! Let's see how they manage when we are away in India. For the present, let's focus on the operations ahead of me this afternoon."

The next few days went very quickly. On Saturday morning, they left for Heathrow airport and caught the afternoon flight to Madras arriving there at 4:00 AM. Three boys and three girls met them at the airport. They all shouted, "Anna!" (means elder brother) and flung themselves at Arun, chattering in Tamil. They did not even notice the others with Arun. Arun extricated himself from their embraces and introduced Liz. They immediately hugged her, shouting, "Akka!" (means elder sister) Liz was embarrassed, despite the warnings given by Arun a few days earlier.

Arun asked them to calm down and introduced Chris, Barbara, and Jessica. The porters took their cases to the minibus, and they got on. The boys and girls took the back seats leaving the front ones for the visitors.

One of the boys introduced himself and others via the mike system, gave a running commentary on the city, and drew their attention to the essential places they were seeing.

What struck all of them was the abject poverty on the roadsides despite the affluence of modern cars and office buildings. The heat and humidity were very high even as early as 5:30 AM, but the bus had a good air-conditioning system. There was so much to see and take in, and none of them had slept well during the flight.

The bus entered a secluded compound, enclosing a large campus. The impressive entrance had an arched signboard: Siva Ashram. Then, like in a stately manor, there was a long driveway leading up to the main building. The bus stopped near the main door, where over 120 boys and girls were waiting. Amidst them, and in the center, was the Head of the Ashram, Guru Siva Iyer.

Liz whispered, "Arun, the place is so huge with so many buildings. Do all the properties belong to the Ashram?"

Arun said, "Our Guru will explain all the details to you. Let us go to the flat reserved for us after meeting the Guru and the welcoming party."

There was pandemonium on seeing Arun, with all the kids shouting, "Anna, Anna," and eager to touch his hands. It was a strange sight to see for the rest of his party. Guruji then hugged Arun, and after a few pleasantries, Liz, Chris, Barbara, and Jessica met Guruji, who said that they should go to the flat and catch up on their sleep. Hot breakfast had been prepared and would be served in the flat by the girls. They would meet again at around 3:00 PM. They all dispersed.

Sita, one of the senior girls, introduced herself and her companions, Radha, Priya, and Nina. She told Liz and the others that for the next four days of their stay they should wear sarees to keep them fresh and a range of sarees in different colors had been left in the flat for them to choose. When they were ready, she and the other girls would show them how to tie a saree. Sita said that for the next 4-5 days, girls would be rotation to show them around and assist them at all times. The girls would have some exposure to British people, their customs, likes, and dislikes.

The flat was a large one on the first floor with four bedrooms, all with ensuite bathrooms, Western-style WC's and fittings. It was well-furnished with a large kitchen, dining room with a 12-seater table and chairs, living room, and front and back verandahs making the flat quite breezy in summer. There was a separate bathroom with a WC for all visitors to the flat.

Liz asked, "Sita, did you choose this flat for us? Are all flats this large in the ashram?"

Sita looked shyly at Arun, and he encouraged her to talk to her Akka, her elder sister.

"Akka, this flat belongs to Anna and is reserved for him whenever he comes to the Ashram. No one else will use it. At his instructions, we prepared it three days ago, for your stay. Anna thinks of even the minute details, and we carry it out. We all are indebted to him immensely." She requested them, "Please freshen up and come to the dining room for breakfast, and then you can all have a few hours of sleep."

The breakfast cooked was South Indian, but there were eggs, bread, butter, jams, and marmalade, with freshly squeezed orange juice, mango, various nuts, and porridge. But they all wanted to taste South Indian food and tried a bit of idli with coconut chutney, Pongal, vadai, and sambar – all spiced very mildly on Arun's instructions.

The ladies enjoyed the hospitality. The girls wanted to accompany them to their rooms to help them unpack, but they wanted to hit the bed within ten minutes of going to their respective places. The girls were disappointed that they could not be of more service but left reluctantly, after saying a few words to Arun in Tamil, the native language used in Madras. The ladies could sense that the boys and girls adored Arun.

When they had all retired to their rooms, Arun told Liz that, for the next few days, he would wake up at 4:00 AM, as is the norm in India, and spend time with Guruji. He encouraged Liz to get to know the boys and girls and the staff in the Ashram.

Two hours later, Arun dressed up and left without disturbing Liz. He went to see Guruji, who was in his room, looking over the accounts. After a brief discussion, he went to see the staff in the Ashram, strolled through the gardens and talked to the gardeners and helpers and then walked into to the various offices, construction sites, schools, kindergarten, colleges, playgrounds, temple and talked to the priests, security personnel, etc. The ladies had got up by then, showered, and the girls had helped them drape their sarees. The girls were so excited that the British ladies were so friendly. All their wrong perceptions of British people slowly disappeared.

At lunch, Arun sat next to the Head of the table, Guruji's seat. The ladies sat with the girls and boys to get to know them. Food was strictly vegetarian, with no onions or garlic. It was simple fare, and the ladies had plenty of help and advice from the boys and girls. Arun finished his lunch within minutes and left with four senior boys to the adjoining room for a meeting. Liz and Chris noticed this and made a note to ask him about it later.

Around mid-day, Guruji asked the ladies whether they would like him to talk about the Ashram – which might take an hour or so – or if they would like to rest again and come down at 3:00 PM for tiffin (cooked snack). The ladies said they would like to hear what Guruji had to tell right away, as they were eager to hear about the Ashram since they left London.

Guruji then asked Liz and Arun to sit on either side of him: Liz to his right and Arun to his left. He said he would explain the significance of this seating arrangement later. During the presentation, boys and girls operated the mike system, the slide projectors, the lights, and the curtains as needed.

He began his narration by welcoming the visitors and, most importantly, Liz 'Akka' to the Ashram. He was pleased that Arun had such a beautiful and talented life partner. Even though their marriage was in a Registry Office, there would be a very short marriage ceremony there this evening between 6:00-7:00 PM, followed by dinner. Four of the girls were assigned to be with the ladies to explain the various procedures. Sita would liaise with Liz, the pretty bride.

He went on to talk about the history of the Ashram. The Ashram, started 30 years ago, was not far from the present campus, by him and his wife as an orphanage in his house. Guru Shiva and his wife Paru (Parvati) had twin sons. Shiva had been a civil engineer involved in the construction of a major dam supervising thousands of laborers, who lived there in huts with their wives and children. Their wives worked too, with month's old babies tied around their backs as they lifted a heavy load of bricks from one location to another. Illness, injury, and death were endemic, leaving many children orphaned. Feeling sorry for their plight, he and Paru began caring for them.

Soon word spread that a friendly family had started an orphanage and unwanted babies could be left there. The couple did not have many servants and could not stop children being left at night. When the project was over, there was no more work. Life grew hard, and food was scarce. There was no aid from the community, and the only way was to go begging for food, morning, and evening. The more affluent people began viewing this as a menace. Slowly, they left the neighborhood, one by one, and his house was the only one left with over 1000 acres of land where nothing grew.

There was a small village nearby with about 200 houses. A few years later, an epidemic of smallpox swept through the town and claimed, in quick succession, Paru, and his two boys' lives. Shiva was left all alone with ten orphans.

When one door closes, God opens another door. Two widowed ladies, Lakshmi and Alamelu, destitute, wanted to join him and help him look after the orphans. He invited them in with folded arms, and both were still with the Ashram.

Guruji narrated, "One night when I could not sleep (usually I lie down on the floor in the front verandah), I heard a sound, and when I went to check, I found a baby wrapped in a towel left by the door. I could listen to the couple talk. They were from a wealthy family, but due to a love affair and succumbing to pleasures of the body, the child was born before marriage. They were from an orthodox Brahmin family judging from the lingua they spoke, in refined, respectful, and sincere in their remorse in not being able to see their baby ever. When I opened the door, they fled.

That orphan was different from the others. He felt begging was wrong. Usually, boys, five years of age, take 3-4 youngsters with them so that people may give them food out of kindness. This boy went to one house and stood outside with his troop. The lady of the house gave two handfuls of rice and one handful of lentils, which he put into different vessels. He continued to stand there and would not leave. The lady got annoyed and shouted, 'Why are you still here? Go to the next house. I have given you food already.'

By then, a good crowd had assembled – one should understand that people did not have any pastimes, and these exchanges were interesting for them to listen to and pass unsolicited comments. The boy quietly said that he wanted food, and he would only accept it if he could do some task for her. He did not want to beg for himself. He said he could sweep the verandahs, polish the shoes, and wash dishes, but he must do to earn the food. His talk touched their hearts – they were impressed by his high thinking. They thought their children would never feel like this while an orphan had noble ideals at this young age.

I heard about this from many villagers, and from that day onwards, all the orphans learned to work doing small tasks and earning their bread. The boy was also very good at reciting Vedas by listening to the priests in the temple, and they took him under their wing and taught him Vedas and Vedanta – two books for all Hindus to read and practice. The slokas in Sanskrit script and many did not know how to pronounce in Sanskrit. Even when they recite a few slokas (songs), they do not know the meaning of what they are saying. It's like, westerners reciting Latin. He spoke correctly and understood every word of it. The boy had a remarkable memory and was quick to learn any language or trade. By the time he was 13, he could speak eight Indian languages and knew a few skills like carpentry, woodworking, machining, electrical wiring, any DIY repairs, and gardening to grow our vegetables and fruits.

He was gifted in his studies and, with the help of scholarships, finally got admission into medical college in Calcutta. The principal and a few professors who interviewed him were very impressed. At the end of the interview, he was still sitting there and, when the principal asked why he was not leaving, he said he had not yet finished. 'I do not want anyone to know I am from an Orphanage,' he said. 'I want to earn and learn. I need accommodation in the hospital hostel and am willing to work when I'm not studying.' They had never met such a candidate, and they agreed to give him a modest salary and light work. Each year his payment increased, and work level also increased. By the third year, he was able to see patients by himself, and, from then on, he was not only able to fund his studies and expenses, but he also used to send Rs. 200 each month to the ashram. This amount, he has kept increasing every year.

When he became a full-fledged medical doctor, he began sending us Rs. 10,000 per month to cover all maintenance and special projects. He arranged to set up a proper kindergarten, primary and secondary school, and a college with all sports facilities.

I'm sure you all know the boy is none other than Arun, the apple of mine, and our eyes. When Arun left for London, they all cried their eyes out, but he promised them he would never cut the umbilical cord. He has not done that. Arun has funded the various projects in schools, buying equipment for the school labs, etc. A unique library was built and had such an extensive collection of books that even the Madras University library frequently borrows books from us.

All our boys and girls are very much in awe of Arun, and they adore him. He was able to bring big companies to recruit our graduates and sponsor their higher education. We have engineers, chartered accountants, lawyers, bankers, investment analysts, and graduates in many specialties. Many of them are well placed and contribute to the Ashram as well.

From a humble beginning 30 years ago, with five orphans, there are now 250 youngsters in the Ashram. All their education is FREE, and for this, we are indebted to Arun. Even though he works in the UK, his contact with us is almost daily, and his planning is thorough. The youngsters are all studying or working part-time within the ashram, which has become a big complex. The ashram itself employs many inmates. Alamelu works as a principal dance teacher and Lakshmi as a Math teacher in secondary school and is the headmistress.

The wearing of uniforms is compulsory, and I'm glad even the ladies from Britain are wearing sarees provided by the Ashram. We have not beaten our drums to attract attention from outside. However, for any functions in temples, large gatherings, weddings in big halls or hotels, the boys and girls help out by serving and assisting, and the payments for these are quite generous. None of them drink or smoke or indulge in drugs, and no tradesmen are allowed inside the ashram. That is why you had to pass through double security gates so that no vendors enter the building. There is a modern shop here to buy all that is needed.

Arun has said that there should be free cycles for people to go from one place to another. These are repaired and maintained in our workshop. He ensured that we were self-sufficient, and all skill levels were available here after suitable training.

There is a nice 100-page booklet about the Ashram tracing our journey from our humble beginnings. The book was the brainchild of Arun, and written by resident journalists, checked by resident proofreaders, printed in the press in the Ashram and sent to select companies who partner us in providing, scholarships, facilities, and training."

Guruji continued his narrative, mentioning a conversation he had with Arun when he was 15 years old. He had asked him whether he missed his parents and whether he hated them for abandoning him. "He emphatically told me, 'No, no, no – never will I hate them.' He said his mother would be crying each night, at least shedding one tear for not seeing him. He said he felt she would be in mental agony but not able to express it to anyone. He only wished she never revealed the truth and enjoyed her married life with her other children.

He said that he passionately believed that the Orphanage had to change so that the children never felt abandoned but formed a strong bond with each other here and with me."

Guruji concluded, "Finally, due to old age – I am 82 years now – I wanted to retire and told Arun so, but he asked me to wait. A few months ago, he said he had found a replacement for me and the change could take place this week. With that in mind, I now introduce the person on my right, Elizabeth, 'Liz Akka' as the new Head of the Ashram."

The whole hall erupted with cries of 'Akka' 'Akka.' Then they wanted a speech!

Liz felt embarrassed and was, for a moment, speechless. But she gamely got to her feet:

"I am at a loss as to where I should start. Arun has pushed a tsunami of facts, feelings, emotions, duties, and responsibilities on me. Firstly, I must thank you, Guruji, for taking such good care of the Ashram – it will be a tough act to follow. I sincerely hope I can rely on your guidance at all stages. We all left the UK thinking it was a holiday trip for sightseeing and enjoying Indian culture and food. It has turned out to be an inspirational experience leading to great responsibility and high expectations from my leadership. I will not let Guruji or you all, and most importantly, Arun, down. With the minute-by-minute directions I will be receiving from him, I can only succeed!

I will be spending the rest of my time here on getting to know you all and put together a core team to be my 'feelers' on various issues. We will go through the entire operations and, with Arun's and Guruji's help, identify many action points for systematic implementation to take this fantastic initiative to greater heights."

There was tremendous applause when Liz concluded. Guruji urged them to disperse and prepare for the Hindu wedding.

When Arun and his group returned to their room, Barbara, Jessica, and Chris wanted to know more about the upcoming ceremony.

Arun explained in brief. "In Indian marriages, there are no bridesmaids, unfortunately. So, there is no role for you, Chris, except assistance while tying *mangalsutra*. The most significant part of the ceremony is the tying of the *mangalsutra*, the pendant of the Gods – this is usually a yellow thread fastened around the neck by tying three knots. The husband ties the first knot, and the sister-in-law ties the remaining two. The thread, after the marriage, is usually replaced by a gold chain. On the wedding day, a *sindoor*, a red dot is placed on the bride's forehead by the husband, and Indian wives wear that symbol every day just like the Christian wedding ring."

Barbara and Jessica were humbled and moved when they heard about Arun's life story and his achievements. They could now understand his commitment to making the village a place for the youngsters to work and stay. They prayed for his further success both in Madras and the town in the UK.

The evening function was part religious and the rest, social. Liz wore an Ashram saree in pale red, and she looked stunning and straightforward. Guruji said that she looked as if the Goddess Lakshmi had descended to wed Arun! These heartfelt compliments quite touched her. The procedures were short, and the *mangalsutra* was tied after Arun put *sindoor* on Liz's forehead. Chris tied the two knots expected of her. As per Indian custom, Arun and Liz bowed down to touch the feet of Guruji, priests, her grandma, and her mum. Passing of their hands over their heads to symbolize their blessings followed this. The priests asked Liz to bow down and touch Arun's feet, but he would have none. A hug from Liz was all he expected.

The dinner menu was quite simple, unlike in Western marriages. There were no meat dishes and no drinks. Arun said that they should never forget that they were in an Orphanage, and no display of affluence was encouraged. Liz made a note of that. She felt she was slowly absorbing the Indian values and was hoping that she would do justice to her new role.

Time flew, and Liz spent the remaining days meeting dignitaries, including the Chief Minister, who promised all assistance, industrialists, and potential sponsors and partners. Everyone was impressed by her beauty and commitment to the cause. She disarmed all with her charming and unexpected, "*Namaste.*"

Back in the ashram, Liz was busy with the core team going over the action points for the next few months. Arun had his plan, which he said he would share with her after returning to the UK.

Sadly, they reluctantly said goodbye to Guruji and all the students in the ashram and left to catch their flight on Saturday morning. They were back in London on the same day and home in the village by nightfall, after a very exhausting but illuminating trip.

EPILOGUE

Arun, a GP in NHS, arrived from India as a fully qualified Medical Practitioner, and his life took a lot of twists and turn in the UK.

He took his family to Madras in India to see the orphanage where he grew up.

There were plans to undertake several community projects in the Village and the small Town in the UK and further develope the Ashram in Madras. It was also Arun's wish that a film would be taken of his life story so far and hoped a producer would come forward to make his dream come true. These are the details, including Chris's wedding, that would be in the 2nd sequel.

.

Lightning Source UK Ltd.
Milton Keynes UK
UKHW041835050820
367766UK00004B/50

9 781728 355009